RENEGADE COWBOY

RENEGADE COWBOY

Nelson Nye

Chivers Press   ●   G.K. Hall & Co.
Bath, Avon, England   Thorndike, Maine USA

This Large Print edition is published by Chivers Press, England and by G.K. Hall & Co., USA.

Published in 1996 in the U.K. by arrangement with the author c/o Golden West Literary Agency.

Published in 1996 in the U.S. by arrangement with Golden West Literary Agency.

U.K. Hardcover ISBN 0–7451–3982–5 (Chivers Large Print)
U.K. Softcover   ISBN 0–7451–4798–4
U.S. Softcover   ISBN 0–7838–1616–2 (Nightingale Collection Edition)

This book was first published as TURBULENT GUNS (London: Wright and Brown, 1940) under the pseudonym Drake C. Denver.

The text of this Large Print edition is unabridged.
Other aspects of the book may vary from the original edition.

Set in 16 pt. New Times Roman.

Printed in Great Britain on acid-free paper.

British Library Cataloguing in Publication Data available

Library of Congress Cataloging-in-Publication Data

Nye, Nelson C. (Nelson Coral), 1907–
    Renegade cowboy / Nelson Nye.
      p. cm.
    ISBN 0–7838–1616–2 (lg. print : lsc)
    1. Large type books.   I. Title.
  [PS3527.Y33R46   1996]
  813′.54—dc20
                                          95–43259

for
Robert Ames Bennett

AUTHOR'S NOTE

The incident forming the basis of the action embodied in Chapter 12 and concluded in Chapter 13 of this novel, found its source in Chapters 18 and 19 of Martin Luis Gunman's 'The Eagle and the Serpent' (Alfred A. Knopf, Inc., New York, 1930), where interested readers will find it more fully treated.

Tortilla Flat, Arizona, 1938

CHAPTER ONE

THE SOLDIER OF FORTUNE

Night silvered the ugly desert and smoothed the roughness of the old stone ruin atop the butte called Satan's Toe. In the abandoned shelter Rio Jack Golden sat sprawled at a rough plank table among dust and cobwebs and creeping things. His elbows, resting on the table's edge, supported cupped hands that held his bristly chin. His gaze seemed lost in the flame of the candle-stump that faintly illumined the dirt and grime, the squalor of his surroundings.

Rio Jack swore, and his strong face twitched. He was weary of life and things which it stood for. Twenty risky hours a day for beans and jerky and rancid coffee. Curtains of dust and the whispering whine of gun-flung lead. Eternal bawling of long-horned cattle thrown wet across the Border. Singing ropes and sudden death. Murder, battle, and swift oblivion. These—all these and more, made the bulky knots in Rio Jack's tally-rope of time for the past four wasted years. These were the things he had lived with, slept with, and damn near died of for more dusty months than he cared to think of.

There was little contrast between Golden and the room in which he sat—so far as externals went. Despite the faint tarnish of degeneration which Neglect had filmed across them both, each was of large dimension, ruggedly built, and thick of hide. Each bore marks of many conflicts.

Golden's rolled-brim hat had once been black—in the days before this madness. Now it was a dirty green, and a chin-strap gave his hard features a tough hombre appearance that was not belied by facts nor the lean white scar that ran along his jaw. His agate eyes, squint wrinkled about their outer corners, peered truculently from a face the colour of shoe leather.

Until now he had known no bitterness at his lot, although left parentless at three. And even now, despite the things that he had seen and heard and the many other things experience had taught him, behind his wide firm lips there lurked a ready laughter—for life, for the world, and for himself.

Beneath his chin-strap's dangling ends a black silk neckerchief was knotted tight about his throat. A dark flannel shirt covered the bulging muscles of his shoulders. Faded blue jeans were stuffed into his high-heeled boots of soft black leather equipped with flashing, big-rowelled spurs.

About his lean-hipped waist dark crossed belts with rows of gleaming cartridges supported greasy Colt-filled holsters which had neither tops nor bottoms—dreaded half-breed holsters from which his worn-handled guns need never be jerked for the purpose of hasty firing.

Rio Jack was wont to describe himself humorously as a 'soldier of Fortune'—a seeker of rainbows and the legendary riches that lay at their tips. Indeed, for the past four years he had been exactly that, though with a sideline he never mentioned. For after all his search included something other than the elusive pot of gold. Something which thus far had proved equally elusive and now seemed to have drawn completely beyond all danger of further pursuit.

A faint sigh slipped from Rio Jack's wide lips as he recalled the last four years. A sigh of regret, one might have thought. And certainly he took no pride in those years, though they had brought him a reputation envied by many men along that strip of land labelled in maps as the 'International Boundary.' A reputation for efficiency in dealing sudden death.

Rio Jack's great laughter rang suddenly through the room. Booming, mocking laughter that shook the spiders' webs along the rafters. And as he laughed, great tears rolled down his wind-burned cheeks.

The man in whose desert hide-out he now was sitting, the man for whom he'd searched four long and bitter years, was dead—killed two days ago he'd learned by a band of renegades across the River!

Four long and dusty years had Rio Jack with unbounded tenacity clung to Ablon's checkered trail. Four years of his life he had willingly thrown away in his grim pursuit of the man who had stolen from him a thing beyond replacement. Four dangerous years had it taken him to uncover this carefully concealed lair of Nevada Ablon's atop the butte called Satan's Toe. Four years—only to learn that while he sat here waiting for the Nevadan's return, the man had been killed by renegade lead across the Border!

An ironic, mocking thought. Yet Rio Jack, sprawled at the rough plank table, laughed at this jest of Fate—laughed till the tears rolled down his cheeks.

* * *

Rio Jack abruptly straightened on the rickety stool. His big body slightly turned in an attitude of listening, he grew taut and rigid as his cat-quick ears caught sounds in the night outside. Caught the muffled thuds and occasional harsh ringing of shod hoofs on the rocky trail.

In the candle's flickering light his bronzed features slowly took on the blank expression of a wooden mask.

The hoofbeats ceased beyond the door. Came the creak of saddle leather, the soft jingle of spur chains, and a muffled thud as booted feet hit earth.

Rio Jack's great frame sagged crouched for action. Yet only the restless stabbing glance of his cold, keen eyes revealed the tension under which he laboured.

For some while there was silence, a dragging hush that was filled with sinister suggestion. Then bootheels clumped with dragging spurs across the space between horse and door.

Inside the crumbling ruin Rio Jack sat waiting on the stool beside the table. As the clumping steps approached the door his big rope-scarred hands dropped their tapering fingers to the half-breed holsters at his thighs; twisted the sheathed weapons till their gaping muzzles bore upon the entrance.

Motionless, he watched the door flung violently open. A girl slipped in, looking back across her shoulder into the moonlit night outside. One small gloved hand reached out to close the heavy door; with the other she raised the long oak bar and dropped it in its slots. Turning swiftly, she started to cross the room. But sight of him brought her willowy body to a stop. Wide eyes searched his bronzed features in a probing stare. He guessed instantly that she had been expecting someone else to occupy the stool on which he sat.

He returned her stare with undisguised amaze. Never had he seen a girl more beautiful than she, nor one in whom the glow of life and youth appeared more fully athrob.

'Expect you're lookin' for Nevada,' he drawled.

'Wrong guess, mister. I'm looking for a hideout.'

'Hideout, eh? We-ll—I expect this here's state property. Help yourself.'

Leaning back against the table he surveyed her with lazy insolence, hands interlaced behind his head.

Her hair was like jet, he saw, where it peeped beneath her dusty cream-coloured Stetson, and in the candlelight it glowed with a soft blue sheen. Eyes of a golden brown stared back at him defiantly, deep pools of liquid lightning in the sun-tanned oval of her face. Tempting scarlet lips that but a moment ago had been parted in surprise, now curled in some expression that he found it hard to place. Beneath an adorable chin her throat curved

6

softly, golden tan to the open collar of her woollen shirt, a covering that but served to accentuate the rounded contours of throbbing breasts and the slim lithe waist beneath them.

Some innate sense of chivalry stirred within him then, prompting him to rise from the stool and whip off his shabby hat in a bow that turned his yellow curls to flowing gold in the candle's mellow light. A slow smile broke through his stubble of yellow beard.

'Seems uncommon odd to encounter a girl like you in the middle of the desert.'

'No law against it, is there?'

'Never heard of any. Kind of dangerous, though, don't you reckon?'

'I imagine it's safe enough—when a gentleman like Rio Jack stands ready to risk life and limb in the cause of distressed femininity,' she mocked.

Rio Jack chuckled. 'You've sharp eyes, Miss—or is it Mrs?'

'It is none of your business,' she answered coolly. 'Is it going to be necessary for me to share this place with you?'

'Don't reckon I've got any strings on you. Leave whenever you've a mind to.'

She drew a deep breath and a touch of anger entered her sun-tanned cheeks.

'Have you any special reason for staying here?'

'Didn't have till about five minutes ago,' he drawled, grinning. 'Not so sure bout that, now.'

Watching her closely, Rio Jack saw her features tighten with sudden resolve. He guessed that she had determined on a plan for getting rid of him and was about to put it to the test.

'Are your guns for sale this evening?'

'How much you offerin'?'

She regarded him coldly. 'What's your price?'

'We-ll—what's the chore?' he countered.

'I'm being followed. I have reasons for not wishing to be stopped. What would you charge to discourage the pursuit?'

A twinkle crept into his hard grey eyes as he looked her over from head to foot. He saw a deep flush stain her cheeks and chuckled. 'Wrong guess,' he told her; 'I'll do it for nothing—*de nada*. Who's followin' you, an' how many?'

'Ten or twelve, I think.' She hesitated, gave him a probing stare, shrugged, and finished: 'Villa's men, most likely. They followed me across the river.'

Rio Jack thought swiftly. Why should any of Villa's men be chasing her? What had she done to earn their enmity? Or was she concealing something on her person which it was vital they should not lose? Whatever the reason for their pursuit, it must be something mighty important, he thought, to bring them into the States.

8

'Where did you cross?'

'Gunsmoke.'

'Hmm. Seems like you'd have been safer right there in town than gallopin' round on the desert.'

An odd light flashed through the golden-brown depths of her glance as it rested in his. 'There were reasons why I thought it safer here. Besides, Pancho has spies in Gunsmoke.'

Rio Jack thought it likely. Even for a border town Gunsmoke, he realized, was uncommon turbulent. A hairy-chested place of itchy trigger-fingers and flashing knives. A good place to steer clear of if one valued one's health. But still, it seemed unlikely that they would dare molest a girl—a girl of her sort, anyway.

'Who's in charge of this bunch—Corva?'

'Escobar, I think.'

'Hmm, the wily Garcia, eh?' Rio Jack grinned through his stubble of yellow beard. Some time had passed since his last meeting with Garcia Escobar, yet he had no doubt but that the fellow remembered him. There was the matter of a broken arm to stir the Mexican's memory. Rio Jack chuckled softly as he recalled the circumstances under which he'd broken it.

'His name seems to amuse you,' the girl remarked. 'He's no laughing matter!'

'Shucks,' he dismissed the Mexican with a shrug.

'Speakin' of names,' he suggested, 'you

9

haven't yet told me yours.'

'You can call me Nita.'

'A pretty name—fits you like a glove.' He paused to listen, head cocked a little to one side as he caught the faint thud of drumming hoofs in the night outside. 'I'm wonderin' if the rest of it would be Ablon?'

She stared, then her scarlet lips parted in a swift tinkle of mirth. 'I wonder.'

'Well, I'd hate to think so,' Rio Jack growled harshly, and, picking up his carbine, started for the door.

'Where are you going?' she caught his arm as he swerved to pass.

He stared down at her and for a moment neither moved. During the interval their glances locked as each sought to read the other's thoughts.

Rio Jack shook off her hand. 'Was figurin' to tackle that chore you give me,' he answered gruffly and, opening the door, stepped out.

* * *

There were a number of things about this girl and her unexpected presence here that he did not understand. But he understood full well the magnetism of her forceful personality.

'A girl in ten thousand,' he muttered as he led her horse to the rickety stable, unsaddled it and led it in beside his own.

'Quit thinkin' about her, you fool!' he

10

upbraided himself as he strode towards the head of the trail that led up the butte from the desert floor beneath. 'She'd never look twice at a gent like Rio Jack. She's folks—an' you're nothin' but another border pistol-hopper!'

At the plateau's brink where the trail went angling steeply down, he crouched in a screen of brush and scanned the moonlit desert where it lay spread out in an endless sea of sand beneath him.

A group of steeple-hatted horsemen sat talking in guarded tones at the foot of the trail. The moonlight glittered on their silver ornaments, was reflected from the carbines slung across their saddles.

Above him the crystal stars twinkled gravely in the cold clear night. Away to the southward rose the deep mournful howl of a lobo. An owl, disturbed by the presence of the whispering horsemen down below, slid past on silent wings.

Rio Jack gripped his rifle and waited.

With his left hand he rolled a cigarette, licked it with his tongue and placed it between his lips. He whipped a match across his jeans; it burst purple and yellow against the drifting shadows, was seen below.

'Who's there?' came a call in Spanish.

Rio Jack smoked in tranquil silence.

Abruptly he saw the Mexicans swing from their saddles, spread out and begin a cautious edging up the trail. He chuckled to himself. He felt that there was an unpleasant surprise waiting for Garcia Escobar. When that salty knifeman knew who crouched with ready rifle atop the trail he would likely wish himself miles away.

This old trail, he mused, must have witnessed many things in its time—sinister things and strange. The sound of sombre farewells; songs and sobbing; shouts and laughter; the rattle of rifle bolts and the piteous groans of departing souls. Well, it would witness some things to-night, he thought grimly, and cuddled his carbine's butt against his shoulder.

'Halt!' his voice rang harshly on the stillness. 'Who speaks?'

'Rio Jack. This trail leads to sudden death, *amigos*. Turn back if you value life.'

Came a buzz of excited whispering, then—

'We would speak with the señorita,' called the voice of Escobar.

'Think again, Garcia. She's gone to bed and left me orders to see that she's not disturbed.'

A muttered curse came up the trail. With startling suddenness bursts of orange flame licked upward from the shadows. The night shuddered to the raucous crash of rifles as whining lead chopped twigs from the brush covert of Rio Jack.

With a rush of booted feet the Mexicans advanced. Shadowy figures leaping from rock to rock, pausing only to fire before scampering

12

to another nearer the trail's top. The night roared as the steeple-hatted riflemen came surging ever nearer.

Yet Rio Jack crouched calmly in the brush, a grim smile hovering just behind the lips that held his smoking cigarette, a steely glint in his hard grey eyes.

He leaned forward abruptly. 'Go back, you crazy fools!'

With a snarling laugh for his answer, Rio Jack squeezed the trigger of his carbine. Again and again he fired at the dodging shadows on the trail, yet with shouts and curses they swarmed constantly nearer.

'Give up the señorita,' came the voice of Garcia Escobar, 'or *Madre de Dios*, I shall stake you to an ant-hill! I shall cut fine strips from your belly and shove them down your throat! With my hands I shall pluck your eyes out and feed them to the vultures!'

'Wind!' jeered Rio Jack. 'You ain't man enough, coyote!'

Swiftly yanking cartridges from his crossed belts, Rio Jack placed them in a little pile atop a rock at his side and sprang to his feet, a levelled six-gun in either hand. Flame belched from their muzzles as the hammers rolled beneath his thumbs.

Groans and snarling curses leaped upward from the trail as steeple-hatted figures writhed, spun, pitched headlong. Others fled wildly, crashing back among their climbing fellows.

For crazy seconds Rio Jack stood upright on the brink, emptying the chambers of his flaming guns into the swirling figures on the shadowed trail, a thin trickle of smoke spiralling upward from the glowing cigarette between his lips.

Suddenly wild panic, born of his uncanny accuracy and fear of his dreaded name, gripped the steeple-hatted renegades. Bawling like frightened cattle, they stampeded down the trail. One man alone turned round to shake a frenzied fist and Rio Jack recognized the distorted face of Garcia Escobar, smuggler, brawler, killer. He sent a last shot winging down the slope, saw Escobar go hurtling backward in a reeling arc to sprawl face down and headlong in the desert's dust.

With broken spirit the renegades dashed for their horses in a mad scramble. Up into their saddles they went, urging their hard-ridden mounts towards the border with quirt and spur as though the devil himself breathed fire and brimstone at their flying heels.

Dropping the butt of his cigarette to the ground, Rio Jack placed a boot-heel on it and went striding towards the crumbling old stone ruin that once had been the hide-out of Nevada Ablon.

'Might's well see if there's any other little things I can do for her while I'm about it,' he mused, wondering who she was and why she had preferred the hazards of the desert to the outward veneer of civilization afforded by the town of Gunsmoke. 'Reckon this night's work has opened an account for me with Villa,' he reflected as he flung open the door and strode within.

He stopped just past the threshold, staring. Then, abruptly, the old place rang to his booming laughter. The girl for whom he had so recklessly risked his life this night was gone!

'The labourer,' he chuckled, 'was deemed unworthy of his hire.'

CHAPTER TWO

GUNSMOKE

The town of Gunsmoke, spawned by border scum, was in its heyday. A rutted dust wallow twisting its serpentine length between two irregular lines of sunbaked adobes and paintless, false-fronted frame structures served for a street and had its beginning and ending in the trackless sands of the desert.

One restaurant, two honkytonks, three stores, a combination blacksmith shop and stable, two public corrals, seven saloons, a court-house and jail, two hotels and eighteen adobe houses, all squatting in the yellow, hock-deep dust, comprised the town.

Three hundred yards south stretched the

sluggish brown waters of the Rio Grande, on the far side of which could be seen the dusty adobes of the Mexican town of Sarizal.

A narrow toll bridge spanned the river. At its north end a small box-like adobe housed the officers of the United States Customs and Immigration departments. At its southern end a similar mud house served the same purpose for the Mexican authorities.

Gunsmoke boasted few permanent citizens other than its merchants and the unfortunate slow-triggered gentry interred in Boot Hill. But its transient population was not only large and turbulent, but was made up of persons of divers bloods and strange mixtures. Americans, Mexicans, Dutchmen, Spaniards, Italians, Indians, half-breeds of all sorts and descriptions.

The town was enjoying its noonday siesta when Rio Jack Golden came jogging in from the desert on his long-legged black gelding. Horses were hitched to every pole in sight, but no inhabitants were meandering along the warped board walks flanking either side of the twisting dusty street.

Rio Jack racked his black gelding in the shade of a long wooden awning fronting the *Sangre de Oro* saloon. After a brief survey of the other mounts tethered to the same hitch rack, he clumped down the board walk to a place bearing the sun-bleached legend *Saloon of the Singing Stopper*, and stepped through

16

the swinging doors into the establishment's cool and dim-lit interior.

Four men playing a desultory game of stud at one of the card tables along the wall looked up and nodded. A couple of hard-faced men with tied-down holsters, drinking at the bar, turned to look him over, and with far greater promptness turned back to their drinks. A bleary-eyed swamper lounging at a table in a far corner peered at him owlishly.

Rio Jack bought a drink, and, leaving the place, sauntered across to the restaurant where he ate a light meal. Returning to the Saloon of the Singing Stopper, he saw that the two hard-faced gunmen had departed.

The men at the poker table beckoned him over.

'Care to take a hand, stranger?' asked a pock-marked man with a star pinned to his greasy vest. 'Jose, here, is figurin' to cash in.'

Rio Jack glanced at the Mexican who was pushing back his chair. 'We-ll,' he drawled, 'I might be persuaded to take a hand. What sort of limit?'

'Sky's the limit,' the sheriff grinned invitingly. 'Draw up a chair an' squat.'

Rio Jack did so, drew a roll of money from his pocket and laid it on the table.

'Currency be all right?'

'Hell, yes!' there was a hungry glitter in the sheriff's eyes. 'Any kind of money goes in Gunsmoke—just so it ain't counterfeit.

Uh—I'm Sheriff Silvas. Fella to yore left is Cimarron Charlie. Fella to yore right is Dagget Pring. Pring owns one of the general stores in this man's town.'

'Glad to meet up with all you gents,' Rio Jack grinned. 'You can call me Rivers—Dusty Rivers.'

Silvas dealt.

'What to you think of the revolution Villa's stagin' over across?' asked Rio Jack presently. 'Think he'll win out?'

Silvas snorted. 'Dunno. Can't say as I give a damn one way or the other. But them ruckshuns across the Rio is sure bringin' a lot of dinero into Gunsmoke.'

'Lot of tough hombres, too, I'll bet.'

'Hell, Gunsmoke don't mind tough articles,' said the sheriff. 'We thrive on 'em. I ain't seen no gents yet in this town that I couldn't handle if I had to. Mostly, though, strangers mind their own business around here. Them as don't can usually be bedded down in Boot Hill.' He chuckled as he raked in the pot, amounting to some fifty dollars.

The deal passed round with Silvas steadily winning. When it came Rio Jack's turn to riffle the pasteboards, he looked at the jackpot that had somehow got started, grinned, and nonchalantly dropped the deck of cards into the nearest spittoon.

Silvas stared, and his pock-marked face grew dark. 'What's the big idee Rivers?'

18

'Well, I'll tell you, Sheriff. Them cards has been runnin' gosh-awful for most of us gents. Take me, for instance. I ain't had no luck at all with that deck.'

'What the hell do I care about that? You got no business throwin' them cards away. I got a notion, by cripes—'

'Then be kind to it,' chuckled Rio Jack, and called to the barkeep for a new deck. 'With blue backs,' he added pointedly. 'The others was red.'

When the new deck was delivered, he broke the seal, peeled off the wrapper and riffled them with no mean skill. Cimarron Charlie cut and Rio Jack made a whirlwind deal.

Picking up his hole card Rio Jack permitted a sparkle to appear in his wide-set agate eyes. The other players, he noticed, appeared to have seen nothing in his expression to alarm them. He chuckled to himself. He had played poker with experts before—and with tinhorns like Silvas.

He wreathed his bronzed features in a disgusted frown. And well he might. He had a jack of spades showing and his hole card was a three of hearts. But he was not discouraged for his opponents did not know this.

He was tackling a delicate thing, but if he could work it right he stood to clean up big. He figured that he had a sight more ready money to put into the game than all three of his opponents put together, and the game was

19

strictly cash for table stakes, with a sky limit for betting.

Silvas had a king of diamonds showing and opened the betting for twenty dollars. Cimarron Charlie threw his two cards to the discard with a surly grunt. Rio Jack stayed for the twenty. Daggett Pring, proprietor of one of Gunsmoke's three general stores, took another peek at his hole card, covered it with his queen of hearts and boosted the bet another twenty.

Silvas shoved in the required twenty and raised fifty dollars more. Rio Jack pushed seventy dollars into the pot and stayed. Pring paid the fifty Silvas had raised him.

Rio Jack dealt another card each. An ace of hearts to Pring, who grinned. A jack of clubs to Silvas, and an ace of spades to himself. Pring, with an ace-queen showing, bet fifty dollars. The sheriff, with a king-jack in different suits, shoved in his fifty and raised two hundred. Rio Jack, with a hurt expression in his eyes and an ace-jack of spades showing in his hand, paid in the two hundred and fifty dollars. Pring licked his thin lips and pushed his owing two hundred into the pot, glancing nervously at Silvas' pock-marked face.

Rio Jack dealt out another card to all hands. A king of hearts went to Pring. A queen of clubs to the sheriff, and a king of spades to himself.

Pring, with an ace-king-queen of hearts showing, bet one hundred dollars. Silvas, with a showing king of diamonds and a queen and jack of clubs; began to look a bit grim. But he counted out the hundred dollars and raised it another hundred. Rio Jack, with a jack-ace-king of spades, paid in the two hundred and raised it three hundred more.

With a chuckle he could not restrain, the thin-lipped Pring shoved in four hundred dollars and raised the pot another two hundred. Silvas shoved in five hundred dollars with an uncertain scowl. Rio Jack paid in his required two hundred, grinned at his two opponents and added another fifty to the bet, figuring that fifty was about all his opponents' pocket-books would allow.

They met the fifty dollar raise and he dealt out the last card to each.

Pring got an eight of spades, which, judging by the angry flush that stained his cheeks, knocked his hopes of victory all to smithereens. The sheriff got a queen of diamonds, making him two queens showing. And unless Rio Jack was figuring wrong, he had a pair of kings as well—one showing and one for a hole card. The card Rio Jack dealt himself was the ten of spades. His cards showing were the jack-ace-king-ten of spades.

The sheriff bet fifty dollars, tentatively; changed his mind and checked the bet, eyeing Rio Jack nervously. Rio Jack shoved five hundred dollars (all he had left) into the pot and grinned expansively.

With a curse, Daggett Pring threw down his cards and shoved back his chair.

Silvas snarled. 'You know I ain't got anywheres near that much left, Rivers! What the hell you figgerin' to do? Freeze me out?'

'It's an act of kindness, Sheriff. You can't beat a royal flush with a pair—or even two pairs. Tell you what I'll do, though. If you can borrow five hundred from your two friends, I'll give you a chance to call.'

'He ain't borryin' none off me, by cripes!' Pring growled. 'I've lost enough in this damn game!'

'Same here,' said Cimarron Charlie. 'Even if I had it, I wouldn't feel like throwin' it after what I've already lost. Looks like you win, Rivers.'

Sheriff Silvas scowled malignantly. 'Hell of a note, I call it, when a gent has to lose all that money jest because he ain't got enough left to call!'

Rio Jack began scooping in the pot. 'You fellows made the rules, not me,' he chuckled. 'You said we was playin' for stakes cash an' present. An' you claimed the sky was the limit in the betting. 'Cording to that, I collect.'

'Like hell you do!' snarled Silvas hoarsely. Reaching swiftly across the table, he exposed Rio Jack's hole card for the three of hearts. 'Gawd, you didn't even have a pair, yuh damn fourflusher! You can't pull no whizzer like that in Gunsmoke, fella!'

22

'Shucks, looks to me like I've already pulled it. Regardless of whether I run a sandy on you or not, you didn't have the dinero to call my last bet. You got no kick comin' a-tall. You bums just picked me out as a lamb for the fleecin' an' got bit your own selves.'

'By Gawd,' snarled Silvas, surging to his feet, 'I got something here that beats a royal flush, whether it's full or bobtailed either!' And his right hand went scooping for his gun.

Rio Jack's hands dropped to his gun-butts and the weapons' naked muzzles jumped above the table-edge. 'Better change your mind quick, Silvas, or you'll sure be one dead shorthorn!'

The sheriff froze, finger-tips almost brushing the notched grip of his sheathed Colt. His jaw dropped and the wild light faded from his close-set eyes.

But his expression of almost comical dismay was not for the speed of the man with the half-breed holsters, as Rio Jack learned the following moment when, from behind his back, a gruff voice said:

'Stick 'em up—everyone!'

Rio Jack hesitated.

'Grab fer the ceilin', damn yuh, or I'll spill your guts!'

Rio Jack's hands rose with the hands of his companions.

'Turn around face-front an' back ag'in' that wall!' the gruff voice commanded.

23

As the four men obeyed, Rio Jack saw the speaker standing crouched just inside the swinging doors, his back to a blank wall. A tall lean man he was, clad in scuffed bat-wing chaps, scarlet sash, black shirt and black sombrero. A black silk neckerchief, drawn tight across the bridge of his nose, concealed all his features save the smouldering dark eyes and a dark bronzed forehead. A weaving gun menaced grimly in either tight-curled fist.

'*El Buitre!*' Pring gasped audibly.

'Glad yuh recognize me,' jeered the bandit. 'Mebbe it'll help yuh behave, knowin' who I am. Wake up there, barkeep an' get a move on! Pony up the dinero yuh got in that bar drawer! *An' don't pull no stunts if yuh want to keep on breathin'!*'

A man thinks swiftly in an emergency that may well mean life or death. Rio Jack was thinking swiftly as he eyed the sinister crouched figure of the masked bandit by the doors. He knew full well how fast he was at getting his Colts in action. But he knew, too, that the fastest hand in the country would have hard work to beat a levelled six-gun in the ready grip of a man who knew its use.

Wisely, he held his hands aloft as did the sheriff and the others.

'Leave the dinero on the bar there while yuh scoop the money on that card table into a sucker bag,' the masked man directed the barkeep.

Rio Jack reflected that it was hard, bitter hard, to stand against the wall with his hands above his head while the barkeep raked the money he had just won into the green sucker bag and moved away with it toward the bar.

'That's right—you've got real savvy, hombre,' El Buitre applauded as the barman scooped the saloon money from the bar and stuffed it also into the bag for the bandit.

'Now just toss that right over here by my feet. An' be right careful that it *lands* at my feet, too!'

'Listen here, fella,' snapped the sheriff. 'You can't get away with a stunt like that in my town!'

'Why not?'

''Cause—'cause—Why, dammit, it's against the law!'

'Oh, have they got law in this damn place?' El Buitre mocked. 'If they have, it's the first time *I* ever heard about it!'

He laughed jeeringly, as, picking up the green bag with his left hand, he began a sidling motion toward the swinging doors. 'If yuh jaspers got a ounce o' sense, yuh won't be stickin' yore ugly mugs outside these doors fer a good five minutes after I leave,' he advised ominously. 'First gent that does won't never know what strikes him!'

'*I* sure won't be stickin' *my* face outside for ten or twenty minutes,' Pring assured him. 'Personally, Vulture, I'm glad you got that

25

dinero off the table 'stead of Rivers, here.'

'Rivers! *Him?* Haw-haw-haw!' the masked bandit guffawed. 'Rivers, eh? That's the best damn joke I've heard in a week. Yuh poor dumb gophers! That ranny is Rio Jack Golden—the Boot Hill Planter!'

A low gasp of surprise went up at the bandit's words. Sheriff Silvas scowled malignantly. 'He is, eh? Well, I'll be havin' a word or two to habla in his ear when you get off the horizon!'

'Treat him rough, Sheriff,' El Buitre chuckled. 'A coupla years in yore buggy jail on bread an' water ought to take some of the salt outa him.'

Rio Jack was staring tensely at the masked robber. How did the fellow come to know his name? he wondered. Many people along the border had, of course, heard of Rio Jack, whose hair-brained exploits were becoming almost legendary. But few indeed were the hombres who might recognize him when they saw him. There was more to this than met the eye, he reflected grimly, trying to place the outlaw's gruff voice.

He would lose that money, and gladly, could he but get a look behind the robber's mask, he mused. But to lose the money and all chance of ever recognizing El Buitre again, should he chance across him without his mask, was bitter hard to contemplate.

'I'll be keepin' you in mind, hombre,' he

drawled.

'That's sure all right with me. If there wasn't so many other guns in this den of vice an' iniquity, I'd sheath these pistols in a minute an' fight it out with yuh, Rio. There never was a Golden foaled that El Buitre couldn't get the best of!'

He backed against the doors, parting them. 'Keep in mind, rannies, that I said five minutes or some fool mountain canary will be gettin' damn bad hurt! *Adíos, amigos.* An' for the dinero—many thanks!'

He backed swiftly through the half-leaf doors. But in doing so, he failed to stoop sufficiently. The high peak of his steeple-crowned sombrero came in violent contact with the lintel. The hat fell from his head, exposing to his startled victims a mane of fiery red hair and a jagged knife-scar that loomed white as summer lightning against the deep bronze of his forehead. The next moment he was gone.

Before the swinging doors had stilled Rio Jack was bounding through them, his eyes two blazing agates, big hands jerking at his guns. *That scar!* Great God in heaven! Hadn't he seen that jagged scar in every dream of the past four years?

As plainly as though he had seen the bandit's face, Rio Jack now knew him for Nevada Ablon!

27

CHAPTER THREE

A NARROW FLIGHT OF STAIRS

Fate often hinges on queer things, and the fate of Nevada Ablon hinged on an odd circumstance as Rio Jack went through the swinging doors of the Saloon of the Singing Stopper in pursuit of him. A swart, hook-nosed giant was bent on entering the resort at the very moment Rio Jack was bent on leaving. Colliding headlong, they went rolling across the narrow porch, down the single step and on to the warped board sidewalk.

They reached their feet at the same instant, and Rio Jack, with a word of swift apology, was about to resume the trail of the fleeing Ablon when the swathy man cracked out viciously with his right fist. The blow caught Rio Jack in the chest, flung him back upon the porch and crashing through the half-leaf doors of the Singing Stopper to fall sprawling on the floor.

He was up in an instant, sheathing his long-barrelled guns as the stranger, hoarse curses rumbling in his hairy throat, came through the swinging doors and at him, big fists clenched.

'Ain't no slat-bellied pistol-hopper in this damn town can shove Bear Paw Klane in the street without gittin' the damn' teeth knocked

28

down his throat!' he roared, and charged.

A swift glance at the grinning faces of Silvas, Pring and Cimarron Charlie served to convince Rio Jack that the hook-nosed Klane had no mean reputation as a rough-and-tumble brawler, and that they expected to see him live up to it pronto. It was a possibility of no great interest to him, however, as he knew considerable of the art of kick-and-bite himself. What did bother him though, was the fact that regardless of which of them might happen to be the victor, Nevada Ablon would by that time have made good his escape. It was a bitter thought.

He side-stepped as Klane came charging in, ripped an uppercut to the swarthy face that sent Klane back upon his heels with a howl of animal rage. With snarling, red-eyed roar, the giant bored in again, both arms flailing.

At the last moment Rio Jack ducked sideways and the giant's whirling fists fell harmlessly across his shoulders. He rose beneath the other's guard, slugged in two heavy chest blows that sent Klane reeling back, striving clumsily to block.

In waded Rio Jack, thinking to follow up his apparent advantage. He found himself diving headlong at a pair of battering rock-hard hairy fists that flung him backward like the kick of a steel-shod mule. Back against the bar he staggered, and the next instant felt two great arms close round his torso as Klane endeavoured to clinch and crush him.

Instinctively Rio Jack's left hand pushed out, found purchase on the giant's chin and shoved. Slowly the heel of his hand forced the swart man's hook-nosed head back and back and back. With a grunt, Klane relaxed his hold, squared off with a strangled curse.

Rio Jack sprang forward. Toe to toe they stood and slugged; crazy, jarring blows that punished while the sheriff and his friends cheered the burly giant on. The thud of pounding fists was like the muffled pounding of a battering ram through the cheers and jeers of Klane's partisans.

But Rio Jack kept his head. If he could get Klane mad enough he knew he stood a chance to win, so he goaded the hairy brawler with drawling taunts between each blow.

'Why don't you hit like you meant it, walrus? A yearlin' kid could slug harder than you're doin'! Fight, you hairy ape! Fight an' quit tryin' to hug me!'

A sizzling oath ripped from the swart-faced giant's lips. A low blow hurled Rio Jack backward with gasping breath, clutching at his stomach, the room spinning crazily in his blurring vision. Through a red mist he saw Klane coming after him, arms outspread like a grasping grizzly. Somehow he managed to straighten enough to take the zip out of the giant's attack with a series of short-arm jabs.

Back and forth they lunged then, slugging,

pummelling in a murderous give-and-take. Rio Jack was panting nearly as hard and fast as was his burly antagonist. They were fairly well matched, both being big and built to endure the terrific mauling each was taking at the other's hands.

Then suddenly Klane stooped low and, before Rio Jack could guess his intention and move to block it, flung his bear-like arms around Rio Jack's thighs, heaved, and sent him hurling over his burly shoulder, to fall with a jarring thud ten feet away. Scrambling up again, Rio Jack ducked sideways just in time to miss Klane's swinging boot. With darting hands, he scooped his pistols from the floor and sheathed them with a blur of motion.

As he straightened, Klane's right fist smashed him in the mouth, battering lips and drawing blood. The giant's left fist glanced off the side of his head but knocked him sprawling on the floor.

Over and over he rolled, twisting, trying to rise, Klane following, kicking savagely at his ribs, his chest, his head. Rio Jack got to his hands and knees. Klane kicked him down. Rio Jack rose again. Klane jumped his back, began riding him with his spurs.

Rio Jack in desperation threw himself over backward. Across the floor they rolled, kicking, slugging, gouging, while Klane's partisans cheered with grinning faces.

Blood-smeared, sweaty, Rio Jack got a hand

in the giant's mane of hair while his other pounded the snarling face. Klane slugged wildly at his stomach until, forced by the giant's gruelling fists, Rio Jack let go his hold and twisted free, finding himself beside a table at the side of the room.

Klane reached his feet first, caught a bottle Silvas threw him, sent it whizzing at Rio Jack. It struck him in the side and bowled him over, sent him sprawling under the table.

Through blood-smeared, half-closed eyes, Rio Jack saw Klane dash towards him with lunging strides and guessed his intention instantly. The giant was going to spring atop the table and send it crashing about his ears.

With an almost superhuman effort he writhed from under just as the leaping giant came down upon the table's top with a crashing jar that smashed it into kindling.

'That brother-in-law of yours is sure some fighter, Silvas!' chuckled Pring with hearty glee.

So it was the sheriff's brother-in-law he was fighting, Rio Jack reflected grimly, as he struggled to his feet. A sweet mess that poker game had left him in for. Already he had the sheriff down on him, and if he licked the burly Klane it was a lead-pipe cinch his life wouldn't be worth the dirt in an elephant's toe-nails if he dared tarry in Gunsmoke-town!

He backed away as Klane sprang with arms outstretched from the wreckage of the table.

'Quit doin' circus stunts an' fight!' he taunted the giant, grinning with battered lips.

Drooling hoarse invective, Klane scooped up a chair and charged. Rio Jack sprang behind a table, tipped it forward and ducked as the chair sailed over his head to crash splintering against the farther wall.

Wrenching a leg from the flimsy table, Rio Jack made for Klane as the man glanced wildly about him for something else to throw. Silvas hurled a bottle and as Rio Jack ducked Klane wrenched the table-leg from his grip and brought it down across his shoulders, knocking him to the floor.

With the room reeling crazily in his blurred vision, Rio Jack drew back as Klane's booted foot swung past his head. Reaching desperately, he got a grip on the giant's other leg and sent him crashing down beside him.

In an instant they were locked in each other's arms again, fighting like beasts of the jungle. Rio Jack pulled a handful of black hair from Klane's thick mane. Klane hooked a finger in a corner of Rio Jack's mouth and pulled at his split lips till the hot blood gushed. Over and over they rolled, twisting, squirming, kicking.

Again they were on their feet. Rallying from a jolting barrage of thudding lefts and rights, Rio Jack, weaving, ducking, crouching, beat Klane back across the room. Silvas, Pring and Cimarron Charlie ducked out of danger from the flying fists. Silvas stuck out a booted foot and Rio Jack, unable to dodge it, went crashing down again. Klane's boot caught him in the chest as he was rising, flung him back against the bar.

Gasping, clutching at the bar with bloody fingers, Rio Jack pulled himself erect, thrust out his foot as Klane came bellowing in and sent him doubled-over backward.

Rio Jack swayed against the bar, striving to get his breath, his green hat hanging to his neck by its chin strap, his features bruised and bloody, battered; his black shirt ripped and torn half off his back.

A long-bladed knife flashed in Klane's right hand as he sent it streaking across the space that separated them. Rio Jack swayed lower and the blade zipped over his shoulder shattering the big mirror behind the bar.

Rio Jack reached back and got a long-necked whisky bottle, two-thirds full. Working the cork out with his teeth, he took a big swallow and hurled the bottle as Klane staggered towards him, the table-leg swinging in his right hand. The bottle missed and Klane came on.

Rio Jack dropped to the floor as the table-leg cut the air above him. He caught the giant behind the knees, heaved upward. Klane went over the bar head first, taking a shelf of bottled liquor with him.

The barkeep popped his head above the bar, a sawed-off shotgun in his hands. Before the man could fire, Rio Jack grabbed it by the barrel and deflected its aim. The blast of buckshot peppered the ceiling. Powdered adobe showered down in a foggy mist, through which Rio Jack wrenched the ugly weapon from the barkeep's hands and hurled it at Silvas.

He heard Silvas swear as, whirling, he caught the bartender by the wrist and with a swift tug yanked him across his bar. Clutching the screaming offender with both big hands, Rio Jack swung him aloft and sent him crashing into Silvas, Pring, and Cimarron Charlie who were rushing towards him with clubbed six-guns. His booming laugh rang out as the four went down in a swearing, kicking, squirming tangle of arms and legs.

Battered and bleeding from a score of cuts and scratches, his black shirt gaping in tatters across his hairy chest, Bear Paw Klane was staggering around the end of the bar. Rio Jack saw a weaving gun in the giant's shaking right hand as he advanced.

'No slat-bellied, yaller-haired bastard kin do what you done tuh me an' git away with it!' he snarled, and cocked his weapon.

Instinctively the hands of Rio Jack dropped hipward. His thumbs rolled back the spurred hammers of his long-barrelled triggerless pistols without removing them from their half-breed holsters. Flame belched from their muzzles and he saw the hairy Klane pitch forward

35

on his face.

Whirling like a cat reversing ends, Rio Jack crashed a fusillade of lead above the hatted heads of Silvas and his friends as they were getting to their feet. Up went their hands like the stuffed limbs of string-jerked puppets. Consternation stamped their faces as they found themselves looking into the muzzles of his guns.

With his weapons trained upon them, Rio Jack went lurching towards the rear door that opened off the end of the cedar bar.

Flinging a pair of final shots into the floor at the sheriff's feet, he kicked the door wide open with his boot and went lunging out. The hot glare of the afternoon sun struck down upon his bare head like a fiery hammer as he sprinted for the front of the saloon.

Jamming fresh cartridges into his smoking weapons, he saw with a scowl that ten horses were racked before the resort. Ten horses— and not one fast-looking bronc among them!

Much as he hated to 'borrow' one of the crowbait nags racked before the resort, Rio Jack disliked far worse the thought of dashing the length of that board walk in an effort to secure his own where it dozed beneath the wooden awning of the Sangre de Oro. Bad as these mounts were, he decided, one of them would have to serve.

Speed and plenty of it seemed the main essential to an immediately prolonged

36

existence. With scant qualms at the probability of a horse-stealing charge being levelled against him by the pock-marked Sheriff Silvas, whom even now he could hear clumping after him with his cronies at his heels, Rio Jack slipped the knotted reins of a claybank mare, swung into the saddle, and with a dash of the spurs went pounding down the street, raising dust hat-high behind.

Whining lead sang past his forward-hunched shoulders as the bark of guns rose from the front of the saloon. Shouts and oaths rang viciously through the deserted street, punctuated rhythmically by the pounding hoofs of the borrowed buckskin.

'An' there ain't much chance of circlin' back towards that bridge across the river,' he thought bodingly. 'An' the river's a sight too strong round here to swim. I've got to figure out somethin' an' I've got to figure dang quick,' he added as a glance across his shoulder disclosed the sheriff and his companions clambering into saddles.

Silvas would be after him hot and heavy and immediate for the killing of his hairy brother-in-law, if for not other reason—and there were plenty that Rio Jack could think of. His cue was to lose the pursuit just as fast as the Lord would let him.

Inspiration came to him when he saw a large can ahead of him in the dusty road. Leaning far down from his saddle he caught it by its upright bale. Swiftly he slashed a length of rope from the *reata* on his saddle horn. Tying one end of it to the bale of the can, he twisted round and lashed the other end to the buckskin's tail. Still holding the can in one hand, with the other he knotted the mare's reins to the horn. Dropping the can, he jumped from the horse's back and dashed in between two adobe dwellings on the outskirts of the town.

Away went the claybank mare with the can banging at her heels. So much dust was the combination raising that Rio Jack doubted very much if the sheriff and his posse would realize that he had left the saddle.

And so it proved. Twenty seconds later Silvas, Pring and Cimarron Charlie went rocketing past his place of concealment on the trail of the stampeding mare.

A grin curled the lips of Rio Jack as he watched them go, heading for the desert and applying quirt and spur.

'Somebody,' he told himself, with a chuckle, 'is gonna be dawgone mad when it is discovered that I ain't in that saddle!'

Well, Silvas would be back and he realized that it would go hard with him if found in town when the sheriff returned. Now was his chance to get his black gelding hitched before the Sangre de Oro. So thinking, he bent his steps in that direction.

But just as he had almost reached the resort, he heard a voice call his name from the mouth of an alley. Turning swiftly, he beheld the bleary-eyed swamper whom he had first seen seated at a table in the rear of the Singing Stopper. He wondered momentarily as he swung towards the alley what had become of the swamper while he was having his rough-and-tumble with Bear Paw Klane. Must have slipped out when the excitement started, he thought.

'Say, mister, was yuh anxious tuh catch up with that El Buitre hombre?'

Rio Jack eyed the swamper closely. A human derelict, if he'd ever seen one. 'What makes you think I was?' he asked coldly.

'We-ll, yuh seemed tuh be in a powerful hurry when yuh bumped into that ornery Klane.'

'Hmm. Do you know where the Vulture went?'

'*Do* I? Mister, for ten bucks I can tell yuh where he is this minute!'

'Sorry,' said Rio Jack, 'but I haven't got ten bucks to my name. The Vulture cleaned me when he robbed the Singin' Stopper.'

He did not put much stock in the swamper's claim. The fellow was likely the same as the majority of his breed; willing to do or swear to anything that required but little effort on the off-chance of gaining drinks or easy money.

But as Rio Jack swung away towards the hitch rack beneath the wooden awning, the swamper sprang forward with unexpected

39

energy and caught him by an arm.

'Listen, mister! If yuh'll promise me that ten bucks when yuh gits it, I'll put yuh wise tuh where yuh can find El Buitre in less'n two minutes!'

Rio Jack gave the little fellow a probing stare and slowly nodded. 'All right, *amigo*. You tell me where the Vulture is an' if I find him there an' don't get killed in what follows, I'll see that you get the dinero.'

The swamper showed his snaggy teeth in a feline grin. 'C'mon,' he grunted, and led the way towards the back of the Sangre de Oro.

Rio Jack walked along behind him thinking fast. Was this some sort of a trap? he asked himself. Still, he did not see how it could be. The fellow was to get his ten dollars only if he led the way to Ablon in such a manner that Rio Jack was able to get the upper hand. Nevertheless, Rio Jack could not dismiss the notion that somehow things were not exactly as they seemed.

They passed through the rear door of the Sangre de Oro, walked down a narrow hall which ran the length of the rear of the building as well as Rio Jack could judge, and came to a door that was slightly ajar. There seemed to be a faint radiance coming from beyond the door.

The swamper placed a hand to his lips. Leaning close he whispered: 'Beyond the door is a flight of steps. They lead to a dugout underneath this joint. El Buitre's got a hide-out down there. I saw him go in jest a few minutes ago without his mask. Don't fergit my ten bucks when yuh gits the best of him.'

Rio Jack nodded, pulled the door open slightly and stared. A narrow flight of stairs led downward as the swamper had said. They were illumined by a burning lamp bracketed to the wall.

'You're sure El Buitre's down there?' he whispered, and started to turn.

He caught the flash of a descending gun-barrel, but not in time to dodge it. Down across his scalp it thumped and everything went black as his knees gave way and he pitched headlong down the stairs.

CHAPTER FOUR

SINGING LEAD

Rio Jack Golden was certainly down—but he was still some ways from being out. The swamper's treacherous blow that had sent him plunging down the abruptly darkened stairs, had done little more than stun him. Far from being knocked unconscious, he was wildly angry when he found himself piled up at the bottom of the flight.

But gradually the hot roaring blood of anger drained away, leaving him with a mind both

41

cold and clear. His bronzed, long-fingered hands were at his hips as he got himself afoot. For breathless moments he crouched silent, heavily-muscled shoulders hunched a trifle forward, hard jaw thrust forth aggressively. No faintest light of fear clouded the cold grey eyes with which he scanned the shadows.

Crouched listening in the murky gloom, cat-quick ears straining for the tiniest alien sound, more and more he grew puzzled at the entire affair. Why should that damn fool swamper lash him across the head and shove him down these stairs? What was the man's game? What could the fellow hope to gain from such a scurvy trick?

From somewhere beyond the top of the stairs he caught a muffled, mocking laugh. The swamper's? Or that skunk, Nevada Ablon's? Booted feet retreated down the hall.

His big fists clenched. He vowed ominously that it would go mighty hard with someone when he got out of this blasted hole! He would take pleasure in teaching those hair-brained nit-wits that Rio Jack was no safe man with whom to monkey!

But the present moment, he reflected with a saturnine grin, was hardly the occasion to dwell upon reprisals. Right now all his energy should be devoted to finding a way out of his predicament. So thinking, he stretched forth his hands and found a door. His heart bounded when he discovered that it was unlocked.

Grasping the knob with his left hand, he pushed the door slowly open. Stygian darkness met his probing gaze.

Rio Jack's left hand sought the snakeskin band of his shabby green hat, found a match and dragged its head across his Levis. It burst crimson against the drifting shadows, showing a long timbered room with a floor of hard-packed earth. A room devoid of human presence.

He advanced cautiously, narrowed eyes stabbing the shadows. There was a dilapidated cot against the farther wall. Hung on nails above it were divers costumes, including the outfit in which he had beheld Nevada Ablon when El Buitre had robbed the Singing Stopper.

His eyes leaped at sight of it. This was Ablon's lair, all right. One of his lairs, at any rate.

Advancing to the cot, he saw a candle stump on a cracker box nearby and lit it. Breaking his burnt match with the characteristic caution of the true range man, Rio Jack dropped it to the floor and began a hasty examination of the garments hung upon the wall. There was a mirror beneath a pile of them on the cot.

At the foot of the cot he noticed a pail of water and a much-used bar of soap. Swiftly stripping the torn shirt from his broad back, he took off his hat and neckerchief and bathed his lacerated face and torso. The smarty touch of the warm alkaline water refreshed his aching body. After cleansing himself as well as possible, working fast, he dried himself with his tattered shirt and again examined the outlaw's wardrobe.

'Funny,' he thought, 'what Ablon's got all these clothes around here for.' Most of the shirts he found were entirely too tight for his broad upper body. But at last he found a black one that seemed almost a perfect fit. 'It's sure uncommon odd that Nevada would have a shirt here that's such a heap too big for him,' he muttered thoughtfully as he buttoned it on. 'An' them cushions! Some luxury for a polecat that shifts scenery with the rapidity of that hombre!'

It almost seemed as though the wily Ablon went in for disguises.

'Say! that's a thought!' A humorous glint crept into the hard grey eyes as he looked over the El Buitre outfit. 'Might help me get out of this town with a whole skin if I was to put on that Vulture get-up.'

Certainly the promptitude with which Silvas and his *compadres* had shoved their hands on high a while ago proved the fearsome respect n which the citizens of Gunsmoke held El Buitre.

'Be a ripsnortin' joke,' he chuckled, 'was I to get away in Ablon's clothes!'

The shirt was far too small for use, he found, but as it was black like the one he had already borrowed he dropped it on the floor with scant waste of time. Putting his black neckerchief on, he drew it tight about his throat. Stepping into the Vulture's scuffed bat-wing chaps he found the fit quite passable. Nevada, too, was long of leg. He removed his gun belts and tied the scarlet sash about his waist, strapped the belts on over it in the manner affected by the outlaw.

So far, so good, he thought. But what was he to do for headgear? His own green Stetson was out of the question. That would be a dead give-away the second anyone saw it. And Ablon, he remembered, had been forced to leave his black sombrero on the floor of the Singing Stopper. That...

Rio Jack's big frame went abruptly tense. There on the floor beside the cracker box lay the Vulture's black sombrero!

Only one thing could explain its presence satisfactorily: the bleary-eyed swamper of the Singing Stopper was in El Buitre's pay. A spy—a look-out—spotter!

'Of course,' said Rio Jack softly. 'That explains why that sawed-off joker led me here an' shoved me down the stairs.' He nodded slowly, and his lips went grim and bleak.

Picking up the straw sombrero he tried it on. A little tight, but with the chin-strap from the hat he was discarding, it would serve. Effecting the transfer, he pulled the chin-strap tight, its silver concho gleaming in the candle's rays.

Putting on the Vulture's mask, Rio Jack regarded himself in Ablon's fly-specked mirror

45

and a soft chuckle left his lips. 'A trifle broad,' he reflected, 'but no gent is goin' to notice that when he's starin' down my guns.'

Turning from the mirror he straightened swiftly. This was not time to indulge in abstract thought. It was time he was getting out of here if he expected to get out alive.

He moved swiftly across the floor, passed through the door by which he had entered and stepped cautiously up the stairs. He had no doubt that the door was locked, but the possibility did not worry him greatly. He believed that he could get around that difficulty without any great exertion. His main fear at the moment was that some unexpected noise or commotion might bring the owner of the Sangre de Oro and his henchmen rushing to the scene. Such an incident might well provide disastrous.

From a hip pocket of his Levis he produced a curiously bent piece of heavy wire. Inserting it in the keyhole of the door he manipulated it industriously until a sudden *click* announced that the lock had sprung. Slipping the wire back into his pocket, he cautiously opened the door, feeling thankful for the price Nevada Ablon must be paying for such privacy.

There was no one in the hall. About halfway down its length he could see a door leading into the bar-room of the resort. He had almost reached it when it opened inward and a man in shirt sleeves rolled to the elbows stepped suddenly into the passage.

Rio Jack stopped tense, shoulders hunched a little forward, arms bent, hands hooked for clenching gunbutts should the man show signs of belligerency.

'Gosh, Nevada, I was afraid yuh'd gone a'ready,' muttered the man in shirt sleeves closing the door behind him softly. 'I got a message fer yuh—here.'

Nodding curtly, not trusting himself to speak with a man on such evidently familiar terms with Ablon, Rio Jack took the bit of paper with his left hand, shoved it in a chaps pocket. 'Ready tuh ride?' asked the fellow. 'Wait, I'll get yore horse. Or was yuh figgerin' tuh use a different one this time?'

There was nothing for it but to answer. To refuse to speak would instantly rouse the fellow's suspicions. Imitating Ablon's voice as well as he could, Rio Jack gruffed:

'Bring round that black geldin' hitched out front.'

The man nodded and stepped back through the door. Lifting the mask a moment Rio Jack wiped the cold sweat from his forehead. Drawing the bit of paper the fellow had handed him from his chaps pocket, he smoothed it swiftly and read:

'I'll be at your place in Sarizal to-night at ten.'

47

The message was signed 'Corva.'

So there was another lair at Sarizal. The Vulture seemed well supplied with hide-outs, thought Rio Jack, his grey eyes growing bleak as agate. Corva, eh? ... Concho Corva, a lieutenant of Pancho Villa! Evidently Nevada Albon was dabbling in Mexican politics besides being an outlaw as a steady trade. 'Fellow must be busier'n a dog with fleas,' he reflected grimly.

At that moment the outer door, the same rear door through which he had followed the treacherous swamper so short a time before opened soundlessly and into the hallway ten feet away stepped Nevada Ablon in person— and without disguise of any sort.

He stopped short at sight of the crouched masked figure behind two levelled pistols. 'Come right in, Nevada,' Rio Jack drawled softly. 'You're just the gent I want to see.'

'Who—who the hell are yuh, hombre?'

'Quit edgin' towards that door or who I am won't worry you very long. Close it, an' be right careful it doesn't slam,' ordered Rio Jack.

Ablon reached towards the door and the next moment was ducking out. Not daring to fire, for fear of attracting unwelcome attention, Rio Jack sprang after him. No sooner had he stepped outside than he saw the outlaw springing to the saddle of his black gelding, the barman staring with bulging eyes from Ablon to the psuedo-El Buitre.

With a squeal of fear, the man in shirt sleeves clawed for the gun in the waistband of his trousers.

It was a poor time for scruples or hesitation. Rio Jack's hands swept hipward. His triggerless Colts belched flame as the hammers dropped beneath his thumbs. He saw the fellow clutch wildly at his chest, stagger sideways and pitch forward in the dust.

Whirling swiftly, Rio Jack blazed lead at the fleeing Ablon, cursed as he saw his slugs fall short. Jamming fresh cartridges into his smoking weapons to replace the bullets shot, he went sprinting towards the hitch rack beneath the wooden awning.

As he jerked loose the reins of a fast-looking pinto, a red-faced man came dashing up. 'Leggo my bronc, yuh dang hoss-thief!' he shouted, and reached for his gun as Rio Jack turned and he saw the mask. Rio Jack's right fist lashed out like a pile-driver and the fellow went over backward with glazing eyes.

Vaulting into the saddle, Rio Jack spurred the pinto down the street, swung him between two adobe shacks and flung him at a dead run towards the open desert. Not sixty yards had he covered when four horsemen topped a distant crest directly in front of him.

Again he changed the pinto's course, swerving to the right. This way led past the rear of the buildings along Gunsmoke's single street that were used for dwellings. A man with a rifle appeared at an open back window. Rio Jack swung low on the pinto's offside as the long gun spoke and the whine of lead cut past the saddle.

Straightening again he drove the pony down a narrow alley between two paintless frames. Straight across the dusty street they plunged and in between a store and a saloon on the riverward side. It looked like the only chance. If he could make the river...

Suddenly the pinto staggered. Kicking free of the stirrups, Rio Jack slid off as his borrowed mount went down in a kicking heap. Lead zipped past his shoulder as he scrambled to his feet, guns in hand, and went zig-zagging towards the open front door of the general store.

Three men were throwing lead from a pair of glassless windows across the street. Rio Jack thumbed four rapid shots, driving the men from sight, then turned and went dashing up the steps to the store porch.

He turned again at the sound of drumming hoofs. The four horsemen he had seen on the desert were now pounding up the street. A bit of metal glinted on the vest of the leading rider. Sheriff Silvas and his posse!

Rio Jack dashed inside the store. A hasty glance showed the place to be unoccupied. Moving behind a counter he pulled a box of .45 cartridges from a shelf and ripped it open. Hastily he jammed the loops of his belts with ammunition. Ejecting such spent shells as were in his guns, he loaded the chambers—full. Shoving up a window then he climbed through and dropped to the ground behind the store.

There was not a man in sight. Three hundred yards away stretched the mud-brown waters of the rippling Rio Grande. Rio Jack headed for the river at a run. Further down he saw signs of activity about the adobe housing the U.S. Customs and Immigration departments beside the bridge; saw two khaki-clad figures with rifles come dashing towards him, shouting.

'Damnation!' Above his mask the eyes of Rio Jack grew desperate as he whirled and went sprinting towards the street again, lead kicking dust about his feet as the men in khaki opened up with their high-powered rifles.

Somehow he made the corner of a building despite the shower of lead and, panting, flung himself around it. Just as he was congratulating himself on his temporary respite, from around the building's front came sprinting Silvas, Pring, and Cimarron Charlie.

'Halt!' snarled Silvas, firing wildly, his bullet whizzing close.

There was nothing else to do. Rio Jack, his retreat cut off from the river, the sheriff and his deputies blocking his advance, resignedly raised his hands.

'Gotcha!' Silvas growled triumphantly. 'Let go them guns, El Buitre!'

Rio Jack dropped his pistols with a sigh.

'What's all the sweat about?' he drawled, with Mexican languor. 'You gents are kickin' a lot of lather up about nothin', looks like to me.'

'About nothin', eh?' snarled Silvas, brandishing his pistol in threatening circles. 'You robbed the Singin' Stopper, shot I don't know how many men, an' now you call it nothin'! Well, *I don't!* I call it a damned outrage—quit wigglin', damn yuh, an' git them hands up high!'

'Reckon I better get his hawg-laigs, boss?' suggested Cimarron Charlie.

'Yeah—pick 'em up afore he decides to fight it out.'

Cimarron Charlie edged up from the side, stooped, and stretched forth a hand to gather in the supposed-bandit's weapons. But his fingers did not reach them. Rio Jack's right boot came up in a blurred arc that ended in his stomach. With a *whoof-f-f!* of mingled pain and astonishment, Cimarron Charlie turned a complete parabola and landed with his face in the dust.

Yet even before the deputy struck the ground, Rio Jack was stooping, springing forward. His striking left fist caught Pring on the side of the jaw and knocked him headlong.

A savage joy was welling up in Rio Jack as he whirled, knocking up Silvas's pistol even as flame belched scarlet from its muzzle. There was a gripping zest to this business of battling against long odds, he felt, as he struggled with

52

the sheriff who was doing his utmost to bring his pistol into line with his antagonist. Rio Jack was bred of fighting stock—hardy pioneers— and the tang of Gunsmoke was like a heady wine, surging hot and riotous in his veins.

Then the tide of battle turned. Even as he wrenched the pistol from Silvas's clutching hand, a terrific blow from the brass-knuckled fist of Cimarron Charlie caught Rio Jack in the back and whirled him staggering six feet away. Before he could pull himself together the sheriff and his deputy were upon him. A rain of showering fists beat him to his knees.

'I got the ring-tailed hellion now!' came Pring's rasping voice, and Rio Jack felt the muzzle of a gun in the small of his back—hard!

'I reckon you have,' he admitted.

Handcuffs were snapped about his wrists as Silvas and Cimarron Charlie jerked him to his feet.

'Here's one damn Vulture what'll get his wings clipped pronto!' the sheriff snarled, shoving him towards the jail. 'One more break outa you, hombre, an' you'll wish you'd never been borned. I got all of your change I'm a-wantin'. Head for the jail an' trot fast!'

Rio Jack flashed Silvas a sharp look above El Buitre's mask. He wondered if the sheriff really thought his prisoner was the man who had robbed the Singing Stopper? What *did* the foxy gunsmoke lawman think? And what sort of crooked scheme was being hatched now in

Silvas's wily brain?

Beneath the mask the wide lips of Rio Jack quirked in grim amusement as he noted the frankly-levelled weapon in the hand of Cimarron Charlie, who apparently believed in taking no further chances with a prisoner as full of kinks and salt as the man in El Buitre's clothes and mask.

CHAPTER FIVE

'YOU'LL HANG TO-NIGHT!'

Arrived at the county jail, a thick-walled adobe building housing not only the cells for the prisoners but the office of the sheriff as well, Silvas dropped into the chair behind his desk and mopped his pock-marked countenance with a bright red bandanna. His close-set eyes took on a hostile glare as he regarded Rio Jack.

'If you got anythin' to say, hombre, git it off'n yore chest quick!'

No sign of fear lighted the cold grey gaze of Rio Jack as he returned the lawman's stare. It was Silvas's glance that finally dropped.

Why had not the sheriff sought to remove his mask? he wondered. Did the Gunsmoke lawman suspect that his prisoner was not El Buitre? It was an unpleasant possibility, and no mistake. Bad as it was to be caught as the wily outlaw, it would certainly be much worse to be so-convicted.

Cimarron Charlie was standing beside the door. It was noticeable that he still held his gun in hand. It required no clairvoyance on the part of Rio Jack to realize that the surly-faced deputy would shoot upon the slightest provocation. He sized up Cimarron Charlie as a quick-trigger gent out to build himself a rep as a bad-man buster, and guessed that he was the sort who preferred to do his shooting at such stubborn outlaws as refused to buy 'protection.'

Pring was standing beside the barred window across from the sheriff's desk. There was a scowl on his bony, red-skinned face and his skinny hands were deep-thrust in his coat pockets.

A fine scrape he'd got himself into this time, thought Rio Jack morosely. He had thought by arraying himself in the Vulture's clothes to escape from the mesh of difficulties attending the poker game and the subsequent fight with Bear Paw Klane, the sheriff's brother-in-law.

But, far from aiding him in his hoped-for getaway, El Buitre's garments had but brought him into fresh difficulties. In fact, his position was far worse now than formerly.

'Nothin' to say, eh?' Silvas growled. 'Can't you think up any lies?'

'What's the use? You wouldn't believe 'em anyway. Why waste your time?'

'Vulture, you hit the nail smack-dab on the head when you said that! I wouldn't believe you on a stack of Bibles ten feet high!'

'Quit gabbin',' gruffed Cimarron Charlie. 'Let's shove the ornery son in a cell an' git it over with 'fore he makes another break.'

'I thought you was hopin' he *would* try some stunt so's you could pot him,' sneered Silvas malignantly. 'Trouble with you, Charlie, is you're light on brains. Always view a situation from every angle, then tackle it from the one that promises the biggest profit—that's my motto. Never go off half-cocked.'

Cimarron Charlie scowled but apparently was unable to find a suitable answer. He began polishing his gun-barrel on a sweaty sleeve.

'Take the Vulture's mask off, Pring, an' let's get a look at his homely mug.'

Pring advanced from behind, reached out cautiously and jerked the black neckerchief down off the face of Rio Jack. The latter's bronzed countenance showed no slightest flicker of emotion as he met the sheriff's startled stare.

'Well,' rumbled Silvas. 'Well! Went fishin' fer minnows an' caught a whale!'

'Never mind the flattery,' jeered Rio Jack. 'You knew damned well I wasn't El Buitre. What's your game?'

The sheriff's sullen mouth betrayed surprise. 'Game? 'Fraid I don't git yore meaning', Rivers—or would you rather I

56

called you Rio Jack?'

'I don't give a damn what you call me,' Rio Jack answered flatly. 'All I'm interested in right now is learning' what you're figuring to arrest me for.'

'Ho-ho,' chuckled Silvas. 'Well, I'll tell you. I always aim to be obligin' whenever possible. I'm arrestin' you fer bein' El Buitre, first of all, naturally. Next, I'm chargin' you with the murder of Bear Paw Klane, a barman at the Sangre de Oro, an' woundin' a couple other gents. Third, I'm arrestin' you for disturbin' the peace. Then I might charge yuh with robbin' the Singing Stopper,' he added, musingly. 'May think of some other things later on. But them'll do fer now.'

'Think of everythin', don't you?'

'Me, I'm thorough,' Silvas bragged.

'You're goin' to have a hard time provin' I'm El Buitre—seeing that I was standing with you boys in the Singing Stopper when he robbed it,' Rio Jack pointed out. 'Don't think you can make those murder charges stick, either. Both them gents was clawin' for their smoke-poles when I dropped 'em.'

'Shucks,' Silvas grinned unpleasantly. 'I wasn't figgerin' to make any of them charges stick—don't figger it'll be necessary. A mob an' a rope necktie will tend to you, young fella!'

Rio Jack stared at the lawman's pock-marked face with its sullen mouth and close-set, red-rimmed eyes. The man was not fooling,

57

he reflected sombrely. He meant just what he said. And he looked ornery enough to do it, too.

'Pretty slick,' he admitted. 'Won't be much profit in it, though.'

'Well, I got a proposition, Rio. If we can come to a deal, I'll see that this don't go no further.'

Rio Jack's ragged yellow brows arched upward. 'Let's hear it, hombre.'

Silvas eyed him narrowly.

'Hell,' sneered Cimarron Charlie. 'Why waste time tryin' to make a dicker? He won't stick to it once he gits loose, anyhow.'

'S'pose you let me do the thinkin' for this outfit,' Silvas growled. 'He'll stick if he agrees to. It's like this, Rio,' he went on, returning his gaze to Golden. 'You got yore good points. You got a rep as a fast gun-slinger. I need such in my business—an' I ain't talkin' about sheriffin', either. There's a number of deals I got in mind that can use a fast gun. Cimarron here is out; he's too well known around Gunsmoke. But you ain't. Togged out as El Buitre, you could work wonders. I'll boss things; you'll tend to the shootin' end. We'll split seventy-thirty. I'll take the seventy an' pay all expenses. How about it?'

''Fraid you might try to double-cross me, Sheriff.'

'That's the chance you'll have to take,' Silvas grinned. 'Howsomever, the only alternative you got is a mob, a rope, an' a cottonwood limb. You damn nitwitted fool, you'll hang to-night fer the killin' of Bear Paw Klane!'

CHAPTER SIX

THE DYING COWBOY

Rio Jack Golden, seated on a wire cot in the dismal county jail, peered through the formidable iron grating at the two men coming down the corridor. One was Sheriff Silvas. His companion was a grey-haired, stoop-shouldered man who munched steadily on the great cud of tobacco reposing in one side of his wrinkled, moustached face.

Elbows firmly planted on chaps-clad knees, square chin in cupped hands, Rio Jack sat with his big frame hunched forward, his hard grey glance unreadable as agate.

'Well, Vulture, you changed that stubborn mind?'

'Not yet, Sidewinder,' Rio Jack grinned with battered lips.

Silvas scowled, turned to his companion. 'Like I told yuh, Judge, this fella's a damn' hard case. Plumb onregenerate.'

'Ask him what he done with that money he stole from the Singing Stopper.'

'Speak up, fella. You heard the Judge's

59

question. Where'd you put that dinero?'

Rio Jack laughed dryly. 'You know well enough I didn't hold up the saloon, Silvas. Why keep up the farce?'

'Worst damn' liar I ever met up with, Judge,' growled the sheriff. 'Don't matter, though. I got three men besides myself that'll swear in any court in the country that this El Buitre hellion stuck up the Singin' Stopper this afternoon at three. Four of us was in there when he sailed in and hollered fer us to pony up all cash. There was me an' Pring an' Cimarron Charlie an' the barkeep.'

The stoop-shouldered man stopped chewing long enough to say: 'I believe you, Sheriff. This young man seems a very obstinate sort. Has he refused right along to admit his guilt?'

'Plumb from the start,' said Silvas, with an oath.

'Hmm. He certainly doesn't look like a killer—except for his eyes. You've noticed his eyes, Sheriff? Rather murderous, aren't they?'

'I never saw a meaner pair, Judge. An' the way he gunned pore Bear Paw! Never give him a Chinaman's chance! Bear Paw was a mite slow in gettin' his hands up, an' this hellion jest let go at him with both pistols!'

'What the hell is this—a game?' growled Rio Jack.

'Game?' The stoop-shouldered judge spat tobacco-juice from the side of his mouth and regarded him curiously. 'I'm afraid you'll find

60

it is rather an unpleasant sort of game before you're through, young man. Instead of being so stubborn and brazen it would be far better for you if you threw yourself on the mercy of my court and made a clean breast of things.'

'Oh! I'm to get a trial, am I?'

'Certainly you'll get a trial,' said the judge with some asperity. 'This county never hung a man yet without giving him every possible chance to prove himself innocent. Your trial, young man, is scheduled for eleven o'clock to-morrow morning.'

'Too bad I won't be here to view the august ceremony,' Rio Jack remarked, ironically.

'What do you mean by that?'

'Honest John Silver here informed me a while ago that I'm to be guest of honour at a lynchin' bee this evenin'.'

'Plumb delirious,' sighed the sheriff. 'He must have got hurt worse'n I figgered durin' that scuffle we had when we put the bracelets on 'im this afternoon. Reckon we ought to have Doc take a squint at him?'

'Don't hardly seem worth while,' the judge said seriously. 'We'll be hanging him to-morrow. No sense in running up a doctor's fee for the county on a man that'll have to die anyway.'

'Reckon that's so, too,' Silvas nodded. 'Well, I guess there ain't much use talkin' to him, Judge. Seems bound an' determined not to admit a thing. We caught him in the very

61

clothes with which he stuck up the Singin' Stopper. Even to the mask. Don't hardly seem necessary to get him to admit anythin' when we got so many reliable witnesses that'll swear to seein' him commit the things I'm gonna charge him with.'

'Mebbe you'd better just charge him with the murder of Mr Klane, Sheriff. That will expedite matters considerably and make for less chance of a slip-up.'

'Whatever you say, Judge. I always wanta do what's right.'

'I know you do. I thank God every night that this county has such a reliable, square and honest sheriff looking after its interests. There are not many counties that can boast of an officer like you, Mr Silvas.'

'You said a mouthful that time,' grunted Rio Jack.

The judge shook his grey head sadly. 'I guess you were right, Sheriff. It seems an utter waste of time to talk with such a hardened character longer. He's one of the hardest cases I ever hope to see. I certainly hope you or your brave deputy, Mr Cimarron Charlie, will be able to locate the money he stole from the Singing Stopper.'

'So do I,' Silvas muttered. 'We was playin' cards when he stuck us up. I was several hundred ahead. I sure hate tuh think of losin' all that dinero. I expect he got away with several thousand bucks, all told.'

62

'Well, perhaps he'll reveal its hiding place before morning, Sheriff. At any rate, let us hope so.'

'Humph, I doubt it. Let's go get a drink.'

'Drink a couple for me, while you're at it,' grunted Rio Jack. 'After listenin' to you two gassin' here for the last half hour, I feel like I could do with several.'

'A hard, hard case,' repeated the judge in sorrowful tones as he and Silvas moved down the corridor.

'Absolutely onregenerate,' the sheriff agreed.

Once more left alone, Rio Jack scowled glumly. Silvas was certainly hellbent on leaving nothing to chance, he reflected. One way or another it seemed very likely that a certain Rio Jack was due to hang before much more water slid beneath the bridge of time. Donning El Buitre's garb had certainly placed him in a mighty unenviable position, he reflected grimly. Unfortunately this Gunsmoke jail greatly differed from the various Western 'jugs' he had so often heard described. Its bars were of solid iron, deep-seated in cement, and try as he would and did, he could find upon them no slightest trace of rust or weakness.

Too, hot weather apparently was no different from cold weather to the sheriff. The single window of his cell was nailed down, and there were bars about the glass both inside and out. And they were solid case-hardened iron rods.

Altogether, it was a rather dreary prospect with which Rio Jack found himself faced.

He had heard of a number of outlaws who had burned themselves out of cow-country jails with the aid of matches carelessly left in their pockets by the searching authorities. But there had been nothing careless about the search Cimarron Charlie had given him. He had cleaned every single thing from the prisoner's pockets and had placed the entire result of his methodical search on the sheriff's desk. Even if he had been left a couple of matches, Rio Jack reflected, they would have offered no means of escape, for the roof and the walls of this building were of adobe—and very thick.

'I'd like to have a word or two with that gent who said "iron bars do not a prison make,"' he grunted sardonically. 'Reckon this must have been one jail he never visited.'

He scowled as he recalled the message to El Buitre given him by the barman of the Sangre de Oro. He would have liked to have done a little searching for the outlaw's lair in Sarizal, would liked to have been present at that rendezvous set for ten o'clock to-night.

'No use reflectin' on that now, though,' he mused. 'By ten o'clock I'm right liable to be decoratin' a cottonwood branch, as the estimable Silvas so cheerfully pointed out.'

He wondered what the sheriff had thought

64

of Corva's note. Possession of that incriminating bit of paper certainly clinched the case against him as El Buitre. Silvas really had no need to incite a mob in order to get rid of him. By merely letting things take their natural course in the trial the judge was contemplating in the morning, enough evidence could be produced to 'send him down the road' for more years than he cared to contemplate.

But the judge had not been intending to try him as El Buitre, he recalled. He was to be tried for the killing of Bear Paw Klane. Certainly with the aid of his perjuring witnesses, Silvas should have little trouble in convincing a jury that Rio Jack had deliberately murdered the fellow.

'Must be in an all-fired hurry to get rid of me,' he reflected, 'if he can't wait till to-morrow.'

Cimarron Charlie came slouching down the corridor with a plate of ham and eggs and a cup of steaming coffee. Stooping, the deputy thrust them beneath the iron grating. 'Eat hearty,' he growled. 'This'll be yore last meal on this planet.'

'You're mighty good to me, Charlie. I didn't think Silvas would see any sense in wasting grub on me, being as he's all set to get me hanged soon's it gets good an' dark.'

''S what I told him. But he said we had tuh do things shipshape. All damn foolishness, if you ask me.'

'By the way, Charlie,' drawled Rio Jack, picking up the plate and cup, 'I wonder if Silvas would mind steppin' back here a few minutes. I'd like a word with him.'

'He's out tuh supper. I'll tell him when he gits back. Won't do you no good, though. He give you a chance tuh throw in with us an' you turned him down. He wouldn't lift his li'l finger tuh save you now if you was the last durn pistoleer on the border.'

Rio Jack just grinned. 'Well, you tell him I want to talk with him, anyhow.'

* * *

'Was you wantin' to see me, Vulture?' asked Silvas, peering through the grating.

'Seems like it's about time you got busy primin' your mob to do its stuff.'

'Gettin' impatient, are you? Well, don't fret. I'm takin' care of it in my own way, fella. Thorough—that's me!' Silvas grinned. 'I hear there's a heap of talk goin' on in the saloons right now. Seems like you're kinda *on*popular in this man's town, Rivers.'

'That's a trouble I have,' Rio Jack lamented. 'People either want to run right up an' hug me or else they take a violent dislike to the way I part my hair. That's the way it was with you, I reckon, wasn't it?'

'Yeah. I don't like the way you part yore

hair, nor the slant of yore eyes, nor the cut of yore jaw. I don't like the damned Mex rig you're wearin' nor the way you play poker. In fact *I plain don't like yuh!*'

'Too independent for your taste, I reckon.'

'You hit the nail right on the head! There's only one boss in Gunsmoke—that's me!'

'"The crowd cheered an' stamped it's feet,"' Rio Jack quoted, grinning. 'Sorry I ain't a crowd, Silvas.'

'Huh! You needn't feel so chipper, fella. You got about one more hour to live. When they put the hemp around yore neck, I guess likely you won't do no cheerin', neither,' growled Silvas, 'but you'll be makin' plenty motions with yore feet!'

'Speaking of motions,' chuckled Rio Jack, 'I make a motion you call this business off before you get yourself in trouble.'

'Kinda late in the day fer threatenin', ain't it?'

Rio Jack's straw-coloured brows lifted mockingly. 'Is it? I didn't know it was ever too late to mention the danger of stringin' up a U.S. Marshal.'

Silva started, then snorted incredulously. 'Shucks, you can't saw that off on me, fella. We looked over yore belongings right careful. There wasn't no badge or papers among 'em. Only paper you had was a incriminatin' message from Concho Corva, the Mex bad-man. Nope, that bluff won't wash, Vulture.'

'Well, I figured I might as well find out, as the old woman said when she kissed the bull.'

'Humph! You'll find yore sand has run out when that mob gits a rope round yore blasted neck,' growled Silvas ominously. 'What was you carryin' that piece of bent wire in yore pocket fer?'

'A hatpin, mebbe.'

'Think you're funny, eh? Well, lemme tell you somethin', smart guy. You'll be a damned sight funnier to me when they cut you down off'n that cottonwood branch you're gonna decorate in about an hour! If you're through with them dishes, shove 'em under the gratin'. Bein's they don't use such things in hell, you won't be needin' 'em any more!'

Saying which, Sheriff Silvas turned on his heel and clumped off down the corridor.

'Cheerful jigger!' mused Rio Jack, returning to his seat on the wire cot. 'A regular Sunny Jim.'

An hour left to live. It was not a great deal of time, he reflected. Too bad they had found that piece of wire. With that he might have extricated himself from his present difficulties—temporarily, at least.

He stiffened suddenly, got slowly to his feet, and, bending, began to examine the cot. Gosh, if he could get one of these little pieces of wire loose, he might even yet make a get-away.

With infinite labour he finally worked a small section loose. A piece about six inches in length. But when he tried to bend it to his needs he found it entirely too stiff. It would bend, but not enough.

Nevertheless, he tried his luck. But the lock successfully withstood his greatest efforts and at last he threw the wire aside with a disgusted grunt.

A glance through the window showed him that it was rapidly getting dark. The saloons and honkytonks farther down the street had lighted their lamps already, and from one of them came the faint strumming of a guitar.

He listened a moment with an ear held close to the closed window. The fellow was playing 'The Dying Cowboy.' He could just make out the words:

'Oh bury me not on the lone prairie,
Where the wild coyotes will howl o'er me,
Where the rattlesnakes hiss and the mosses
    wave,
And the sun beats down on a cowboy's
    grave.'

Rio Jack moved away from the window with a growl. 'I hope to hell he busts a gut!' he muttered, and slumped down on the cot again.

It was hard, bitter hard, to realize that there was absolutely nothing he could do to help himself. His act in putting on the Vulture's clothes had walked him into a trap, and now the trap had got him. Try as he would, he could

69

see no way out.

For dragging minutes he wrestled with his problems. Out of the maze of his thoughts, one solid truth came hammering at him insistently. He was done, washed up. Nevada Ablon would go swaggering along his path of crime and depredation while Silvas and his surly deputy dug a hole for him among the silent denizens of Gunsmoke's Boot Hill.

Rio Jack's square jaw jutted defiantly. Let Silvas stir up his damned mob! Let them come and get him! He would die as he had lived— fighting! No *reata* would haul *him* off the ground! He would raise so much hell with that mob that some impulsive gent would shoot. Well, let him. Better by far to die from a bullet than with his feet kicking out his life from the end of somebody's strangling lass-rope.

His grim reflections were disturbed by the sound of voices from the sheriff's office. Surely the crowd was not worked up sufficiently this soon to enjoy its entertainment!

He strove to catch the conversation. Two people were talking, he judged; one of them sounded like the surly deputy, Cimarron Charlie, but the other voice he could not make out. Nor could he catch any words. Judging by the tones and inflections, the deputy was arguing, protesting against something being proposed by the other speaker.

The door of the sheriff's office abruptly opened, throwing a faint glow of light across the floor. Booted feet thumped out an approach. In his cell Rio Jack caught the faint sound of dragging spur chains. He braced himself for fight should this prove a visit from the lynchers.

'Unlock this cell,' a soft whisper pulsed through the gloom. 'Rio Jack won't hang to-night.'

He leaned forward in an attempt to see his rescuer's face. But the murky shadows lay too thick and he could make out nothing except a blurred shape behind the grumbling deputy. Whoever the fellow was, he must be menacing Cimarron Charlie with a gun to obtain such fine results, he thought as a key grated in the lock and the door swung slowly open.

'I'm sending Charlie into your cell,' came the whisper. 'Better gag an' tie him.'

'It'll be a pleasure, pardner,' grunted Rio Jack, and swung his right fist in an arc that ended with a dull thud behind the unsuspecting deputy's ear. Cimarron Charlie promptly lost interest in the events going on and dropped limply to the floor.

Swiftly Rio Jack lashed his wrists behind his back, using the deputy's belt for the purpose. Using his neckerchief—the black one he had lifted from the Vulture—Rio Jack gagged the deputy in such a manner that it would be some time before Cimarron Charlie employed his vocal cords again.

'Here are your gun belts and your pistols,'

71

the unknown whispered.

Strapping them about his waist, Rio Jack felt a glow of exultation surging up within him. They would have a tough fight on their hands if they tried to lynch him now, he reflected as he followed his rescuer down a diverging corridor that led to a side exit.

Opening the door, the unknown whispered softly: 'Listen!'

Through the hush of early evening came the rumbling tramp of many booted feet and the low growl of guttural voices. Silvas's threatened mob was on the move!

CHAPTER SEVEN

'KEEP YOUR DAMN' HANDS OFF!'

Rio Jack's gray eyes grew hard and shiny. Great cords of muscle tightened along his jaws. Thought of the man responsible for the arousing of that dread monster stumbling towards the jail caused his big hands to open and shut convulsively. A whisper of escaping breath came from his parted lips.

In the faint starlight seeping in through the open door he saw that his masked companion was regarding him curiously.

'*Oyes los truenos, coyote?*' came the sibilant whisper—'You hear the thunder, coyote?'

'Yeah,' he answered, 'I hear it. But if it's

72

your notion I'm a coyote, seems uncommon odd you took the trouble to snag me clear.'

'I pay my debts,' returned the masked one, cryptically. 'Time we got in motion. Under those junipers over there,' a gloved hand indicated the spot, some three hundred yards away, 'I've cached horses. Crossing that open stretch may be a bit ticklish in case we're seen. Mob will probably be headed for the front of the jail. We'll walk casually as though we had all day to get where we're going. Ready?'

But before Rio Jack could frame an answer, a rasping voice from the sheriff's office shouted: 'Hey, Cimarron! Where the hell you at?'

'Silvas!'

Rio Jack's breath sucked in harshly as he nodded. An oath formed on his tight pressed lips and his hands dropped down to leather. The icy glint deepened in his eyes. But he did not draw.

'Quick! Out the door!' came the whispered command. 'Then take it easy till we reach the junipers.'

'Somethin' ought to be done about that damned sheriff,' Rio Jack muttered. 'He'll speed that mob with his loud shoutin'—'

'No time to bother with him now,' cut in the masked one. 'Come on.'

Out of the door they went, closing it behind them softly, then moving with leisurely unconcern towards the distant clump of trees

73

while the sheriff's muted cursing filled their ears with wrath and their minds with dire foreboding.

Thirty, forty sauntered paces they took before an enraged shout announced the sheriff's discovery of the trussed deputy and the escape of his prisoner.

Prickly chills shot up the spine of Rio Jack. Only the utmost straining of his stubborn will prevented his booted feet from breaking into a run that would have given them away to the nearby mob converging on the front of the jail.

Nerves of iron must be possessed by his masked companion, he thought, so nonchalantly did the fellow gait their progress. It was their only chance, of course, yet it seemed impossible to Rio Jack that his slim companion should have such marvellous composure in the face of that steadily-advancing mob and the sheriff's bellowed wrath.

Once the masked man half-turned as though to retrace his steps and seek the cause of disturbance. Then he shook his head, moved on a few paces and actually stopped. He seemed to be scanning the ground. Suddenly he stooped, reached out a gloved hand as though picking something up, grunted, and made a motion of throwing it away.

They moved on then, unhurriedly resuming their way towards the deeper shadows of the junipers, while Rio Jack wiped cold sweat from

74

his forehead. He glanced covertly at his unknown rescuer. Here, he decided, was a man to tie to, a fit hombre with whom to ride the river.

'Better pull that neckerchief up over your face, Vulture. Might's well both be masked, while we're about it. How you feeling?'

'Hellish,' admitted Rio Jack, and took no shame in the admission. 'Pardner, you've got sand in your craw.'

'Shucks,' was the whispered answer, 'I've been in heaps pinchier tights than this.'

Rio Jack said nothing. He could find no suitable retort.

They had approached within a hundred yards of their objective when a sudden commotion swept the crowded street before the jail. The slam of heavy doors, shouts, curses and the slog of booted feet told them that the mob had been informed of their escape. An ominous growl arose that drowned all other sounds. A hasty glance across his shoulder showed Rio Jack that the mob was spreading, fanning out to take up the search.

A sudden cry sheered through the early night. 'There they go! After 'em boys!'

With a roar the mob sprinted for the junipers. Rio Jack and his companion ran for the now-discernible horses tethered beneath the trees.

A spatter of shots crashed out as they reached the deeper gloom, jerked loose the

75

horses' reins and vaulted to their saddles.

'Which way?' rasped Rio Jack.

'Head for the river.'

'They'll stop us at the bridge.'

'Don't try for the bridge—we'll have to swim the river.'

'The current's too swift an' there's quicksand bars,' objected Rio Jack. 'We'll never make it across.'

'Quit arguin' an' fan your bronc!' snarled the other. 'The river's our only chance!'

'You're the doctor,' grunted Rio Jack, and dug in the spurs. Like grey wolves they sped from beneath the junipers, pounded out across the sand, the stranger's dun gelding in the lead.

'There they go!' yelled Silvas's raging bellow. 'Five hundred dollars apiece to the gent that drops 'em!'

Bullets whined through the night. Gun-flashes blossomed luridly among the shadows. With dripping spurs and swinging quirts the fugitives raced for the silvery gleam that marked the Rio Grande, while shouts and curses rose from the pursuing mob.

Flying lead cut through the crown of Rio Jack's chin-strapped sombrero. Lead tugged at the slim leader's vest, and jerked the wind-blown scarf at his neck. But neither rider swerved nor slowed his pace.

Rio Jack risked a flashing look behind. The liquor-bolstered mob, broken now into running, leaderless units of shouting, swearing pursuers, was still coming. Even as he looked, Rio Jack saw two horses break from the running ranks, rapidly leaving them behind. He guessed instantly that the two riders were Silvas and Cimarron Charlie. And they were coming fast.

The screen of willow brush that marked the river's bank rushed swiftly nearer.

The water, Rio Jack saw as they approached, was a roaring, whirling torrent. He sensed instantly that there must have been a cloudburst further up. Driftwood of all sorts and sizes was being borne along on the angry surge.

'Can't make it here ... try further down!' shouted his slim companion, and swerved his horse.

Along the bank they pounded. A glance behind showed Silvas and his deputy striving desperately to head them.

Abruptly the masked unknown swung his horse into the willow brush. Rio Jack crashed through behind him, ducking as the pursuing lawmen unlimbered their pistols. Here, he saw in a fleeting glance at the foaming current, a crossing was just within the realms of possibility.

Swiftly he pulled his guns from their sheaths, shoved them into his chaps pockets and buttoned the flaps as an added precaution. He worked off his boots and, with a slice cut from the lass-rope affixed to the saddle, draped them

77

securely to the horn. Looking ahead, he saw that his companion had done the same.

Through the screen of willow brush and into the churning flood Rio Jack drove his mount in the wake of the stranger's. At first his horse shied back, but with a firm hand he forced him on, slipping finally from the saddle.

His recollections of the crossing were a chaotic jumble. He was vaguely conscious of fighting with every inch of his body against the sucking grip of the river. Somehow he managed to keep hold of his horse's tail, though he seemed to be fighting with every finger and every toe for endless ages, struggling against the buffeting, sucking grip of that turbulent, thrashing current of liquid mud. His first coherent remembrance was of feeling more or less solid slime beneath his unsupporting legs which told him that he must have reached the opposite bank.

Swaying, lurching, floundering sometimes even crawling, he drew out of the swirling flood.

He found himself presently lying on the cool sand a score of feet from the reedy shore. There was no sign of his horse. Yet somehow he fetched a shaky laugh. Gone were his horse, his boots and spurs, but it might have been worse, he told himself. After all, he was still alive.

He peered about as well as he could for some sign of the masked youth who had risked his life to save him from Silvas's jail and his liquor-fed lynch mob. He tried to yell, but there seemed no breath left in his body and the beating of his heart was like the battering reverberations of some monstrous gong.

He hated to leave without the slender youth to whom he owed his life. He wanted to search the river bank, but had neither the strength nor the time. He dared not linger here for there was no telling what strings the wily Silvas might yank in an effort to recapture him.

Pulling the pistols from the pockets of his soggy chaps, Rio Jack ejected the cartridges from their cylinders and did his best to dry the weapons with wisps of bunch grass and willow leaves. Finally, having done the best he could with such poor substitutes for a cotton rag, he reloaded them and returned them to their half-breed holsters. Then he kicked off the heavy chaps and struck off across the sand.

Upstream, possibly a mile and a half away, twinkled the distant lights of Sarizal, the Mexican town across from Gunsmoke. He marvelled that the river had not carried him even further, so swift and relentless had seemed its grip.

His bare feet ached intolerably before he had gone fifty steps. The sandy shore was studded with some form of low-lying cactus upon which he seemed constantly stepping. Their needles must have been minute yet they stung like tenpenny nails.

Red and fat the moon peeped above the

low-lying hills to the east, yet its light still gave but scant aid to the multitude of stars glowing like tiny lanterns seemingly but a rope's length above the earth.

As he stumbled through the sand on burning feet, Rio Jack abruptly saw an outstretched shape before him, lying prone.

'Who is there?' came the whispered challenge, and he saw the moonlight glinting on a polished tube extended from a weaving hand. 'Speak quick hombre, or I'll put you to wielding a fork in Lucifer's Legion!'

Rio Jack chuckled softly, despite the gravity of the situation. 'Howdy, Black Mask,' he said easily. 'Didn't think you'd cut the mustard.'

'Oh, it's you, eh? Did your horse make it? Mine was struck by a big log and went under near the middle.'

'Mine's gone, too. Where do we move from here?'

The other pointed with an ungloved hand that seemed strangely white. 'Sarizal. I have friends there who will provide us with clothes and horses. I notice you managed to save your guns.'

Rio Jack nodded, eyeing his companion covertly. The slender youth still wore the black neckerchief mask across the bridge of his nose. Must care a heap more for secrecy than comfort, he thought curiously. The identity of the gallant stripling had been puzzling him for some time. The fellow was certainly cautious;

even now he spoke in a guarded whisper. Well, whoever he was, he had certainly earned Rio Jack's gratitude. He said as much.

'Keep your thanks for those that need it,' he was told loftily.

Independence personified, he thought, grinning behind his hand. For several minutes they lay there side by side, exhausted.

At last the masked unknown got himself afoot, squared his shoulders defiantly, and said: 'Come on. May as well get started. I have an engagement for ten o'clock that must be kept.'

As they trudged along towards the distant light of Sarizal the lightening moon rose higher above the ragged outline of the purple hills. Rio Jack lost sense of time. He seemed to be moving onward in an aching nightmare of physical pain. Struggling, struggling—ever struggling onward, each new step an added misery.

In the vast silence of the border night, only the crunching of his bleeding feet in the coarse sand and his rasping breath, together with that of the limping figure ahead, made sound.

Abruptly the slender leader swayed and stumbled, would have fallen save for the outflung arm of Rio Jack. 'Easy, old man.' He steadied the other with an arm about his waist. 'Better rest a minute. Town ain't more'n a half mile ahead now.'

To his surprise, the masked youth wrenched himself free; turned blazing dark eyes on Rio

Jack. 'Keep your damn' hands off me! When I can't stand on my own two feet I'm willin' to fall!'

To Rio Jack the ferocious whisper sounded very near a snarl. 'Sorry, pard,' he muttered. 'Thought you were goin' to fall—'

'When I get too feeble to make a hand,' the other rasped, 'I'll quit!' and, turning, resumed his limping progress.

Rio Jack lurched after him, plodding painfully in his wake. Funny sort of jigger, he mused. Prideful as all hell! But game clean through.

Some rods they moved across the sand when again the reeling leader stumbled, this time falling flat. Rio Jack stooped above him. 'Can I help you, pardner?'

The motionless figure made no reply.

Rio Jack thought swiftly. The fellow had said he must be in Sarizal by ten o'clock. It must be nearly that now, he thought. There were reasons why he, too, would like to get to town by that time—he had not forgotten the note of Concho Corva and was determined, if possible, to be present at the meeting between the bandit leader and El Buitre. Perhaps El Buitre would not be there, considering the fact that Corva's message had miscarried. There was, however, a notion in Rio Jack's mind that once again he might be able to pass himself off as the Vulture. If successful, he might learn something from the Mexican that would be of

82

decided advantage.

Determined, in the furtherance of this plan, to carry his rescuer if need be, he slipped his hands beneath the face-down figure in the sand. In that crouching position Rio Jack abruptly froze, and a soft oath crossed his battered lips.

Swiftly he turned the unconscious stripling over and slipped the masking neckerchief down about the suntanned neck. Long-lashed lids concealed the wide dark eyes. A scarlet bandanna beneath the hat concealed the jet-black hair. But a tempting pair of slighty-parted red lips lay open to his gaze.

As he stooped there, staring, there was admiration in his glance, and something more. Then the brown eyes flickered open. They were calm with a trace of defiance in their tawny depths.

He stood back and she struggled to her feet. 'Well, what are you going to do about it, now that you know?' she demanded coolly.

'Nita, I—' he hesitated, at a loss for words. The nonchalant daring of this beautiful girl took his breath away. He shuddered as he thought of that angry flood she'd battled. No wonder she had fallen just now from exhaustion. The miracle was that she had ever succeeding in crossing that surging torrent!

'Skip it,' she cut in tersely. 'It's getting late and I must be in Sarizal by ten. If you'll lend me an arm occasionally, I think I can manage to hoof the rest of the way. Can't be more than half a mile.'

'Nearer quarter of a mile, I reckon,' he said. 'Just where is it you want to go? Do you want me with you, or shall I fade soon as we reach the outskirts?'

The girl's red lips curved softly in a fleeting smile. 'I suppose you've earned the right to come,' she answered. 'It is just conceivable that I might need you. I have a brief errand at the Hacienda of the Limping Crow.'

Rio Jack concealed a start. The Hacienda of the Limping Crow, as he knew by experience, was no fit place for a girl like the one before him.

'I'll go with you then,' he grunted. He would far rather be at that rendezvous with Concho Corva, but he realized that he could not very well permit this girl knowingly to visit such a place as she had named without adequate protection. 'How long you figurin' to be there?'

'Not more than fifteen or twenty minutes, I think. I may be able to get you some dry clothes there—a horse, anyway, and boots.'

They struck off again across the sand without further words.

A quarter of an hour later they halted in the shadows of a giant pepper tree. The Hacienda of the Limping Crow lay before them, a long, squat weather-whipped adobe with a balcony along the front. Lights twinkled from the scattered windows. The soft strumming of a guitar drifted out to the watching pair beneath the pepper's fernlike foliage.

CHAPTER EIGHT

IDLE STIRRUPS

'You insist on goin' through with this crazy tryst?' asked Rio Jack, eyeing the squat adobe distastefully.

'Of course.'

'That's a damn bad place for a—a girl of your sort,' he said grimly. 'All kinds of trash hang out in there; half-castes, smugglers, gunrunners, revolutionists—renegades of the worst stamp. Better let me go in with you.'

'I shall be safe enough,' she replied coolly. 'I'd rather you stayed here. The person I am going to meet would not like it if he saw you with me. No telling what form his resentment would take. You will do me a greater favour by remaining here.'

'Will you promise to call if I'm needed?'

She hesitated, but finally gave in. 'Very well, if I find myself in an odious position I will call you,' she said, and started towards the tavern.

Rio Jack was not at all satisfied with the situation. The more he thought about it the more he cursed himself for a fool in allowing Nita to have her way. If she needed him he would be too far away to render assistance in time, he felt. The sky was the limit and anything went inside those adobe walls. The place was a pig-sty.

The hellish music of an automatic piano abruptly drowned the soft strumming of the man who played the guitar. Rio Jack's lips pressed tight. In that infernal uproar he would never hear Nita's voice should she yell her head off, he thought angrily.

Swiftly he stole forward through the dust and shadows. Everything smelled of dirt and filth and whisky. As he drew nearer the air fairly reeked with the stench of unwashed bodies. A guard was slumped against a wall beside the rear entrance. Before the man realized what was happening he felt a gun thrust into his stomach and found himself staring into Rio Jack's masked countenance.

'Off with the boots, *amigo!*'

The guard stared at him as if he thought he were crazy, then bent to pull the scuffed boots with their glittering spurs from his legs. Rio Jack brought his gun down across the fellow's head, just behind the right ear. The man dropped forward on his face without sound other than the soft thud of his fall.

Swiftly Rio Jack pulled the man's belt from his trousers, lashed his hands behind his back. He stuffed the man's filthy neckerchief into his mouth, then yanked the boots from his feet and put them on his own. They were a bit loose, but

86

much better than none.

He dragged the man off some distance from the door, dumping him into a patch of deep shadows. Then slipping his masking neckerchief down round his neck and pulling it tight he entered the tavern of ill repute.

He had no means of knowing which room the girl had been bound for, but guessed that it would be a private one. The only way to make sure, he felt, was to visit them all.

The place was illumined with smoky, evil-smelling kerosene lamps. The atmosphere was clouded with tobacco smoke and foul with the stale odours of whisky and sweaty bodies. As he strolled from room to room ugly prostitutes brushed against his broad shoulders, brazen in their attempts to solicit trade. Their loud cries intermingled with the racket of the gambling machines and the incessant hellish jangle of the automatic piano.

Presently he found himself in a long bare room with white washed walls in which over fifty people of both sexes bent low above little tables, their shining eyes fixed upon an arrangement of placards covered with black figures. A rasping voice shouted numbers in Spanish and English.

He stopped a moment at the entrance of another room, the rear of which, among the groups of vari-garbed men and women, was occupied by green-covered tables with piles of red, blue and yellow chips. Poker, roulette, monte and craps were being played by the ardent patrons.

A swarthy, pock-marked half-breed in tattered cotton pants (which might once have been white) and an open ragged shirt crossed by a heavy cartridge-belt across one shoulder, shuffled up to him dragging a rifle by its barrel.

'Death is one long sleep, eh, *amigo*?' he leered.

'*Quien sabe*—who knows? I have never been dead, my friend.'

'You have somet'eeng to look forward to,' chuckled the swarthy one, poking Rio Jack in the ribs with a dirty thumb. 'Many times 'ave I died, compadre. First at the assassination of Madero. Since that time I 'ave suffered so many deaths I cannot recall them all.'

'You must have been a very great man— perhaps still are,' Rio Jack spoke soberly. 'What are you called, *amigo*?'

'I am Mexico,' muttered the pock-marked one, and lurched away with a rasping laugh.

Rio Jack, staring after the tattered figure, wondered if the man were crazy or if his absurd talk had been a veiled warning. Finally he shrugged and sauntered with a tiny tinkle of spurs from his borrowed boots down a narrow corridor. It was lined with closed doors which he guessed might well conceal private rooms.

A swift glance across his shoulder assured him that he was unobserved. For the moment there was no one in sight. He stooped cautiously and placed an eye at the nearest keyhole in an effort to locate the vanished Nita. He straightened abruptly with a muttered oath. Gambling was not the only source of profit for the Hacienda of the Limping Crow!

Moving to the next door he bent down again. Unfortunately a key on the other side obstructed his view. But his ears picked up a low murmur of voices from inside the room. There appeared to be three persons talking and one of them, he would have sworn, was the girl. Both the other voices were masculine and threatening.

Turning his head sideways, he pressed an ear as close as the protruding knob would permit. A faint grin quirked the corners of his wide lips as he recalled the old saying anent eavesdroppers hearing no good of themselves. He was not interested in hearing about himself just now. What he wanted was to find out what was going on behind the closed door. But only faint words here and there were discernible till suddenly one of the masculine voices raised in anger:

'*Madre de Dios!* You'll hand over those papers or stay here until you rot!'

Rio Jack's big frame grew tense. By his voice he recognized the speaker as the chubby-faced Concho Corva! Evidently he had stumbled on the rendezvous for El Buitre after all—but

89

strive as he would he could catch no sound of Ablon's voice.

*   *   *

Abruptly Rio Jack felt something round and hard pressed viciously into his back. He did not need to see the thing to realize that it was the muzzle of a gun. He straightened slowly and turned around. Framed by a huge hat was the dark face of the pock-marked fellow who had called himself Mexico.

'So here is the way gringos spend their time, eh?'

'I was looking for a friend,' said Rio Jack, his bronzed features reflecting no emotion.

'Yes?' the man leered. 'Do all gringos look for their friends in keyholes?'

At that moment a scream rang out beyond the door. Rio Jack's right foot came up in a swinging arc that sent the fellow's weapon spinning over his head and down the corridor and before the pock-marked one could recover, Rio Jack's right hand drew a pistol and smashed its barrel against the swarthy face. Mexico crumpled.

Yet even as he whirled, Rio Jack heard the door flung open behind him. Corva and another man stood crouched with levelled weapons. Rio Jack realized that he might succeed in shooting one or both, but equally probable was the chance that one of them would succeed in leading him. He raised his hands. The advantage was theirs because they had the girl disarmed and bound behind them.

'Your move, gents,' he grinned.

Corva's chubby olive-tinted face broke suddenly into an expression of recognition.

'Rio Jack Golden!' he whispered.

'Right you are, General—right as usual.'

Corva threw back his slim shoulders at the compliment. A swaggerer was the flashy Concho, his steeple-crowned gold-spangled sombrero chin-strapped to his sleek head at a rakish angle. Beneath his pointed black moustache, his lips curled with mocking amusement. He wore a flowing yellow silk shirt and his nattily-tailored lavender pants were red-striped down the seams. His pistols were silver-chased and his open-topped holsters hand-tooled.

'*Carramba!* but it is the long time since I have met up weeth you,' he chuckled malignantly. 'What are you doing here? Why have you knocked that man down weeth your pistol?'

'Well, it's a long story. I reckon you'd find it boring. What have you bound that girl for?'

'She is a spy!' hissed Corva. 'She has stolen documents of value from us,' he turned a menacing stare upon her, adding: 'But we shall recover them, I can tell you!'

'She may have stolen them,' Rio Jack grinned coldly. 'But she hasn't got them now.'

'No?'

'No.'

91

'Who has then?' Corva demanded, and his companion nodded vigorously.

Rio Jack had been doing some fast thinking. He must extricate Nita from her predicament no matter what the cost to himself. For in the past few hours he had come to find that he was irresistibly drawn towards her, first in admiration for her cool efficiency, then in all things. She was the most desirable girl he had ever met, and the first one who had ever succeeded in rousing his interest.

'Yes,' seconded Corva's arrogant-featured companion who wore a sarape and carried his head high. Like Corva, he wore two pistols, one of which he now held in his right hand, its muzzle trained on Rio Jack's breast.

'Yes,' he repeated. 'If the papers are no longer in her possession, be so kind as to say who has them now.'

'We-ll, I have,' lied Rio Jack, and saw in Nita's eyes—almost black in the lamp light—a touch of approving surprise that he felt more than compensated him for the risk he had deliberately taken.

'You!' snarled Corva. 'How do *you* come to be mixed up in this?'

'That's another long story that wouldn't interest you,' grinned Rio Jack, who took delight in baiting the pompous peacock.

'If it is true that you have them, be so good as to hand them over,' said the handsome man in the broad-brimmed grey hat and long sarape.

'And who the devil are you?'

'My name is Fierro—perhaps you have heard of me?'

Rio Jack turned an appraising stare on the tall Fierro. Who had not heard of this chief aid of Pancho Villa? Merciless, unrelenting, a man with a one-track mind whom nothing and nobody ever held back. To him an order from Pancho was as the word of God—save perhaps that it was more important. General Fierro was he jaguar's paw, the whip, the scourge of the famed Division of the North, commanded by General Villa. A man to fear and avoid as one would avoid the devil.

'Who hasn't heard the name Fierro,' said Rio Jack, 'must indeed be deaf.'

The awe-inspiring figure bowed and a faint smile curled the saturnine lips.

'Then have the goodness, since you know of me, to hand over those papers which you say you have.'

'These papers are for General Villa himself,' countered Rio Jack, and saw a furtive gleam in Corva's eyes. 'When I see Villa I will surrender them, and not until.'

Fierro's thin smile abruptly widened. 'Then you shall have an opportunity to do so shortly. Corva, take his pistols!'

Holstering his own, Corva advanced warily. But he need not have been alarmed for Rio Jack had no intention of committing suicide. And one false move with the glittering eye of

93

Fierro upon him, backed as it was by the man's levelled pistol, would have been nothing less.

'March down the hall four doors and stop,' commanded the general, after Corva had secured the guns of Rio Jack. 'Corva, fetch the girl.'

CHAPTER NINE

PANCHO VILLA

Back in nineteen-ten, as Rio Jack was well aware, the dictatorship of Porfirio Diaz had been paramount in Mexico; liberal, progressive, yet a dictatorship none the less. But the nation had become tired of his eternal candidacy and, wishing to regain control of its civic destiny, had put forward in opposition Francisco I. Madero. Diaz continued in power until Madero headed an uprising, overthrew Porfirio's regime and took over the president's job himself.

Madero, at heart a gentle reformer, preached ideals of justice and professed an undying faith in the triumph of the right. As president, he tried to tone down the revolutionary tendencies of his constituents and divert their energies into safer channels. Thinking to preserve the material well-being of the nation, he refused to put out of gear the political machinery and instruments of the former dictator. He insisted on maintaining the existing army and those in command of it; he enforced the orders of the courts and those whom Diaz had placed in charge of them. He made no changes in the existing legislative bodies and made no attempt to shake up the personnel of government departments. His policy soon proved fatal and lost him the sympathy and loyalty of his friends.

A portion of the army under Bernardo Reyes and Felix Diaz rebelled in February, 1913. Several days later another division, commanded by Victoriano Huerta, revolted after solemn oaths of allegiance. Swiftly these three factions joined forces and Huerta had the revolutionary Madero assassinated.

Public indignation and anger rose to such a fever heat that upon the following day revolution swept the country from North to South. Swiftly the citizens manifested a seething desire to regenerate the entire government.

Venustiano Carranza, governor of Coahuila, was made First Chief of the revolutionary army. The new uprising's political aspirations were set forth in the Plan of Guadalupe, drawn up March 27, 1913.

The new movement was much more general and dangerous than the one headed by Madero. There emerged from the very first four principal centres of revolutionary activity.

In Sonora, Chihuahua, and Coahuila in the north, and in Morelos to the south. The northern troops were led by Alvaro Obregon, who eventually became president, Francisco Villa—the redoubtable Pancho—and Pablo Gonzalez. In the south the revolution's leader was Emiliano Zapata.

At first the advances of the revolutionary forces were slow, mere feeble sparks. But gradually the armies gathered momentum, especially after the fierce battles won by Villa and Felipe Angeles, until they became irresistible. Through such northern states as Sonora, Sinaloa, Nayarit and Jalisco, Obregon marched from one victory to another; from the American border to the very heart of Mexico. Once Villa had succeeded in breaking through Huerta's army, Pablo Gonzalez found himself able to move forward from the northeast. And as Zapata became constantly more menacing from the south, Huerta was forced to flee the country. His flight took place seventeen months after he had ordered the murder of Madero.

After stamping out the last resistance of the one-time forces of Porfirio Diaz and discharging from service all who surrendered, the victorious revolutionary troops moved into Mexico City in the August of 1914.

The revolution then became divided against itself. Carranza, unscrupulous and utterly without ideals, immediately set out to do everything in his means to halt the advancement of every revolutionist of note whose independence, or whose morals and ideals, might later prove an obstacle to his personal ambition. In this he was ardently backed by Obregon. The two did everything in their power to halt the military operations of Villa and Angeles.

Realizing that this internal strife was threatening to destroy all fruits of victory, the various leaders called an assembly of generals and governors. Sovereign authority was voted the Convention in October. The result was that it decided to remove both Villa and Carranza from their commands, as the quarrels of these two formed the principal cause of dissension. General Eulalio Gutierrez was named president *pro tem* of the re-born republic.

Those generals and governors in favour of Villa agreed to the Convention's terms at once. But Carranza and his friends demanded the accepting of specified conditions before they would even consider the Convention's terms. Gutierrez could not consent to their demands, so was forced to temporize with Villa until the Carranza adherents should recognize his authority, which they steadily refused to do.

At last, in December, 1914, Pancho Villa left them flat and took refuge with his soldiers; disowned by the President and at the mercy of Carranza.

And now, in the spring of 1915, the

revolution had degenerated into a clear-cut struggle between Carranza—aided by Obregon and others—and Pancho Villa—each determined by hook or crook to gain the balance of power.

All this was known to Rio Jack, through his four years of dodging up and down the Border in his hunt for the elusive Ablon. During this time he had met many of the general's aides, but had not to date come face to face with the great Pancho himself. But as he strode along ahead of Corva, he felt that he was not much longer to be denied that privilege.

He wondered about the mysterious papers. What did they contain? It was quite possible, he thought, that they might contain a list of prominent civilians who had promised Villa aid, and which would prove their death warrant should the list fall into Carranza's hands. But if this were so, the lovely Nita was undoubtedly an agent of the Carranza-Obregon interests. If this should prove to be the case, it would go hard with her now that she had fallen into Villa's trap.

'Halt!' growled Corva, for Rio Jack had reached the designated door. Fierro thrust the girl forward and, whipping out a knife, severed the rope that lashed her wrists. Stepping in front of them, he knocked upon the door.

A short stocky guard appeared in answer to Fierro's knock. Grounding the butt of his rifle, he saluted in a manner that included all. The brim of his enormous hat, thought Rio Jack, seemed to weigh him down and give him the appearance of being more squat than he was actually. Across his breast there seemed to be ten or twelve cartridge belts stuffed with gleaming rows of shells.

'The Chief is busy,' he said in Spanish.

'Give him my compliments,' said Fierro in a toneless voice. 'Tell him I have two prisoners here that I think he'd like to see. A gringo pig called Rio Jack and that stuck-up daughter of Colonel Guzman, Carranza's infantry.'

Rio Jack could speak Spanish like a Mexican and understood perfectly Fierro's message. But his eyes remained unreadable as agate and the deep strength of him kept his face like a bronze mask.

So Nita was the daughter of one of Carranza's colonels! That explained a lot. Especially when one remembered that since the President had broken with Villa, Carranza was openly determined to put an end to the latter. To Rio Jack, it now seemed certain that the girl was indeed, as Corva had called her, a spy!

Rio Jack was quick to realize that, such being the case, he had risked the Villa wrath needlessly, since sharing the girl's guilt meant the stolen papers seemed unlikely now to do her any service, unless—

The door reopened and the guard's big hat-framed face beckoned.

'Well, come in if you must. The General will

see you. But let me warn you; he is in no pleasant mood.'

Fierro entered first, his tall handsome figure stalking along in his glistening puttees as though he had not a care in the world. And Rio Jack, following with the girl, thought it likely that he hadn't. Corva came last, his pistol held level and ready.

The door opened into a low-ceiled square room with a damp earth floor. A coal-oil lamp, atop a pile of saddles and ammunition boxes, shed dim light and smoke throughout the interior with its cob-webbed, whitewashed walls.

Up and down the centre of the room paced a robust, khaki-clad figure with unbelievably long arms and a bestial gait. 'The damned son of a bitch!' he growled between clenched teeth at every other step. 'The damned son of a bitch! I'll make some extra hats, ~~by God~~!'

He whirled abruptly on one of the officers standing by the wall; 'Go on, friend. You tell that damned fool I don't want him using up the wires on foolish questions. Tell him to shoot the swine instantly!'

The man squeezed by the newcomers, leaving the room in such a hurry he forgot to salute.

The pacing figure stopped to glare at Fierro. 'Well, friend? Make it short.'

Fierro grinned and there was nothing pleasant in the grimace. 'I got two prisoners,

Chief. Look 'em over. Juanita Guzman there managed somehow to get hold of the papers Ablon was carrying, but he sent us word in time for us to arrange a trap and catch her. She claims she hasn't got any papers. But—'

Villa glared at the girl, then turned his blazing eyes on Fierro.

'Have you searched her?'

'Not yet. Just as we were going to, we heard a commotion in the hall. This fellow,' he flicked a thumb at Rio Jack, 'was just knocking Mexico down with his pistol—'

'What for?'

It made Rio Jack's blood run cold to look at Villa then. He was a big man. Beneath the chin-strapped slouch hat, the Mexican's curly saffron locks clustered round his broad curved forehead. The short ends of his tawny thick moustache threw moving shadows across his mouth. The restless, bloodshot eyes came to a glaring focus, staring sharply, and the energetic line of his great under jaw thrust forward belligerently.

Yet nothing, Rio Jack felt, so drew the attention as did the enormous pistol that swung at the general's hip in a huge open-topped holster. Its butt shone with the hard gleam of a thing in constant use. Around both sides of his thick waist ran rows of glinting bullets, whose size, he thought, might not unworthily be compared to torpedoes. But it was that big gun that drew the eye; it seemed a very part of him. And if reports were true, it certainly was.

'What for?' he growled impatiently.

'A matter of expediency, General. The fellow had a gun in his hand. It was pointing my way when I kicked it out of his grip. Just to make sure he behaved, I rapped him with my own. That's when Fierro and Corva invaded the scene.'

'Humph! What were you doing when he pointed his pistol at you?'

Rio Jack grinned coldly. 'I was listening at a keyhole.'

The faces of the officers along the wall registered shocked surprise. Villa stared at the brazen admission. 'This one?'

'No. the one behind which Corva and Fierro there were questionin' that girl.'

Villa's restless tiger-eyes flashed a look at Fierro, who nodded.

'What were you listening for, friend?'

Rio Jack forced a chuckle. 'Curiosity, mostly. I recognized Corva's voice an' the girl's. Wanted to see what was up. You see, I knew she was a Carranzan spy.' He avoided the girl's eyes hoping that she would forgive him later when he had a chance to explain that what he was doing he considered for her own good. For the good of both of them, in fact. He looked at Villa.

The general sat down on the edge of a table that creaked beneath his weight. 'You're a cool one, friend. How did you know she was a spy?'

'Because,' Rio Jack was thinking fast, 'I took away from her a couple of nights ago the papers she stole from Nevada Ablon.'

Villa grunted. Fierro's eyes held a feline gleam. Corva looked incredulous, stood twisting his black moustache. Along the wall the officers stared, one man chewing a toothpick rhythmically.

'So *you've* got those papers, have you? Well, well. This interests me a lot. I ought to wring that swine Ablon's neck for ever letting loose of them.'

He stared sharply, appraisingly, as he asked: 'What do they call you, friend?'

'Rio Jack Golden.'

'Oh. I've heard of you. Fast with a gun, they say. What were you doing here to-night?'

'Heard you were here an'—'

Villa's eyes blazed suddenly. *'You what!'* His face flamed with anger as he jerked out the words. 'How the hell did you hear I was at this place? It was supposed to be a secret!'

'Well, you know how things get around,' Rio Jack evaded, grinning. 'Pretty hard to keep news like that from leakin' out. Pancho Villa's an important man—lots of jaspers interested in his movements, seems like.'

'I got a notion to empty some more damned hats,' Villa's voice was sinister as he glared at the staff officers along the wall, who stared back with stupefied astonishment not

103

unmingled with fear.

'Well, go on, friend,' said Villa, returning his gaze to Rio Jack. 'You heard I was here.'

'Yeah. An' as I wanted to get in touch with you about those papers I recovered for you, I came over here to look you up.'

Villa nodded his tawny head slowly, but Rio Jack caught a glint of disbelief in the slanting glance of Corva. He wondered if Fierro, too, was suspicious. But his smiling eyes gave no indication of his fears to the others as he waited for the general to speak.

'Well, thanks, friend. I appreciate that. Where are those papers, now? Have the seals been broken!'

'*Nada*—seals are still intact. But,' added Rio Jack slowly, 'I haven't got 'em with me. Didn't dare bring 'em when I wasn't sure of finding you. Didn't want them gettin' into the wrong hands again.'

'Where you got them?'

'Got 'em cached at a place in Gunsmoke—not right in the town, you understand, but out a piece on the desert where any curious hombre will have the devil's own time findin' 'em.'

'How long'll it take you to get them for me?'

'That's a question,' Rio Jack said dryly. 'That fool Gunsmoke sheriff is after my scalp. Comin' through there to-day I had to shoot a couple of friends of his an' he slapped on his war paint heavy.'

'Well, I got to leave here in the mornin','

Villa said. 'Could you get them for me by nine o'clock? I'll make it worth your while to run the risk, friend. I need them papers bad.'

'Well,' Rio Jack appeared to hesitate. It would never do to let these fellows think he was in a hurry to get away. 'I'll tell you what, General. I could use some money, I'll admit but I'd get more pleasure out of joinin' your army than out of any dinero you could hand me. So I'll do my damndest to get them papers for you if you'll make me some sort of an officer. Could you do that?'

'Could I do it? Hell! It's done,' Villa said in a tone that was half rough, half affectionate. 'You're a man after my own heart, friend. I'll make you a colonel of cavalry. But, remember, I want them papers by nine o'clock in the morning!'

'You said it, General,' Rio Jack brought his spurred heels together and saluted. 'Can you fix me up with some clothes and a bronc before I leave? I lost my nag crossin' the river to-night.'

Villa stared. 'You crossed the Rio Grande? You're one brave fellow, friend!' He swung his restless eyes on Corva. 'Outfit him, Captain, and see that he gets the best.'

As Rio Jack started for the door, Fierro said: 'What about this girl, General?' and Rio Jack saw that his glance held a hungry gleam. A gleam that boded ill for Nita should Villa give her in charge of the sinister Fierro.

105

'A damned Carranzan spy, eh?' Villa eyed her silently a moment, then his face flamed with anger as he turned back to Fierro. 'What about her?' he shouted wrathfully. 'What a question! What the hell do we usually do with spies? Shoot her, of course!'

Fierro blinked. 'Very good, General,' he said, and grabbed Nita by the arm.

'Just a minute,' Rio Jack cut in, 'I don't think I'd shoot her offhand that way, General.'

He shivered inwardly as Villa's blazing eyes swung round, but no muscle of his face betrayed him, and his agate eyes were steady as he returned the other's stare. 'I'd think that over a minute first.'

He saw that the officers along the wall suddenly shut their eyes. Plainly Villa was not used to having his commands disputed. His face flamed with a terrible rage as his right hand drew his big pistol, pulling back the hammer with his thumb.

'Now say that to me again,' he invited.

The muzzle of the gun was within two feet of Rio Jack's face. Above the sights he could see the furious glitter of Villa's eyes. The lamplight brought out a glint of copper about their brilliant whites and the enamel of his teeth gleamed like polished ivory. The vision of death came more from those glaring fire-flecked eyes than from the gaping orifice of he pistol's barrel, he thought. Neither the eyes nor

106

the weapon altered their gaze a fraction. Without turning his glance from the pistol, Rio Jack saw that there was a leering grin on the face of Fierro.

'Say that again,' Villa gritted.

Not by the flick of an eyelash did Rio Jack show fear. 'I said,' he drawled, 'that I don't think I'd shoot the girl if I were you.'

CHAPTER TEN

'I'LL LAY YOU OUT COLD!'

Villa suddenly chuckled. Returning his pistol to its sheath he looked at Fierro and asked:

'A game bantam, this one, eh?'

No one answered, nor did Villa seem to expect a reply. Turning back to Rio Jack he asked, returning to his seat on the table edge, and in a voice calm with a strange contrast to his stormy tones of a moment before:

'Let's see. Why don't you think I ought to have her shot?'

'That,' answered Rio Jack, feeling suddenly shaky now that the danger seemed to have passed, 'is something that I would prefer to tell you without an audience. I am sure these other gents could have no interest in my motives.'

'Alone, eh? Well, friend, I think I will take you up on that. Corva, have a fast horse made ready at once. Then bring to this room—' he broke off, turning back to Rio Jack. 'Do you want a uniform or something else?'

'Somethin' in the vaquero line would be O.K. for the stunt I have in mind, I guess. I don't reckon I could get across the bridge with one of your uniforms on, an' I sure don't want to swim the river a second time to-night.'

'Well,' Villa said to Corva, 'get him a vaquero's outfit, then. He's got broad shoulders, so get a big one. And be sure to bring his pistols back. He might need them before he rejoins us.'

As Corva left the room, the general turned to Fierro. 'Clear the room, pal. You can wait in the hall. Take the girl with you and see that she don't get away.'

As Fierro was about to go out the door, in the wake of the others, Villa added; 'And you better change the guard. This fellow heard about me bein' here to-night. Maybe some of Carranza's swine know about it, too. I don't want to get shot.'

Nodding, Fierro went out and closed the door.

'Now, why don't you think my order was right, friend?'

'Because,' said Rio Jack, slowly. 'I think she'll be more use to us alive.'

'Hmm.' Villa buried the fingers of his left hand in the reddish tangle of hair that hung over his forehead, and scratched. 'More use alive than dead, eh? You mean we might use her to take false information to the despot?'

'Yeah. We could arrange it somehow so she could overhear some false information, an' fix it somehow so's she could get away without suspicionin' that we were deliberately lettin' her. That way you might be able to lead some of the reactionary troops into a trap where you could blast hell out of them.'

Villa was listening with his mouth a little open, his face wearing that mechanical smile that seemed to start at the edge of his teeth. Now he nodded.

'Thanks, friend. That's a damned good idea.'

'An' anyway,' added Rio Jack, driving in his final argument, 'you couldn't lose nothin' by letting her go, because the seals on them papers are still intact, provin' that she don't know what's in them.'

Villa nodded and his restless eyes went towards the door. 'Fierro!'

The general thrust in his head.

'Put that girl in the next room and post a guard outside the door.'

'Corva's waiting.'

'Send him in. Send my staff in, too, pal.'

'You've changed your mind about shooting that Guzman?' Fierro seemed disappointed, though it did not show in his voice.

'Let's say rather that I've decided to postpone her death until morning,' Villa

109

winked at Rio Jack, whose wide lips parted in a grin.

Corva entered the room, followed by the staff officers. He handed a bundle of clothing to the man who had changed the general's mind, then proffered his triggerless pistols which Rio Jack gratefully placed in their half-breed holsters.

Ten minutes later Rio Jack looked like a different person. On his head was the broad-brimmed hat of a *charo*, effectively concealing his yellow curls. Beneath his tight jacket, a shirt of scarlet silk covered his broad shoulders. Tight doe-skin trousers with slashed bottoms encased his long legs, and his soft leather boots were equipped with flashing, big-rowelled spurs. Swiftly he strapped his gun belts about his lean waist, over the scarlet sash he had donned.

'Bravo,' cried Villa, approvingly. 'That sheriff will never know you now unless he gets close enough to peek into your gun-muzzles, friend. *Vaya con Dios*. And be sure you are back with those papers by nine o'clock.'

Rio Jack, podded, though he had no notion of leaving the vicinity of the Hacienda of the Limping Crow until he should see Nita also on her way. He saluted, hoping it would be for the last time, and went out, closing the door softly behind him.

The long hall was deserted save for the sentry who stood before the door of the girl's

110

room. Recalling abruptly that he had forgotten to ask Corva where his horse was being held, he turned and put the question to the guard.

'By the rear entrance, *señor.*' Saluting, he added: 'It is tied to a post. A big sorrel gelding.'

With jingling spurs Rio Jack strode down the hall, humming softly.

Just as he came within sight of the rear entrance, however, a man stepped inside, saying something over his shoulder to a man outside. The steeple-crowned hat turned.

Rio Jack's gray eyes narrowed as swiftly as the newcomer's widened in startled surprise. The fellow's shirt was open nearly to the waist, disclosing a dirty bandage about his chest—a bandage he was wearing because of a bullet sped two nights ago by Rio Jack. For the fellow blocking the door was Garcia Escobar, the renegade who had led the border ruffians in their attempt to capture Nita that night on Satan's Toe.

There was no time for hesitation. Already Escobar's clawed hand was dropping towards his belt.

The speed-blurred hands of Rio Jack closed round the grips of his pistols. The hammers dropped beneath his thumbs. The twin reports lashed up the churning echoes. Escobar doubled up, clutching at his middle. Slowly he dropped to hands and knees in the centre of the passage. There was blood in his sobbing cry.

Rio Jack vaulted his shuddering figure,

111

sprang through the doorway and landed crouched and ready in the moonlit yard outside. A startled peon stood beside a sorrel gelding, his eyes almost popping from his head at the sudden apparition.

Rio Jack knew that the course of wisdom dictated that he kill the man instantly before the fellow, realizing what had happened, sounded an alarm. The sound of the shots themselves meant nothing, since shooting was a common occurrence at the Hacienda of the Limping Crow. He knew that he ought to kill the man, yet he did nothing of the sort.

Leaping forward almost on the instant of seeing the peon, Rio Jack brought a flashing gun-barrel down across the fellow's throat. The peon reeled backward without a sound and his arms flung out grotesquely as he fell outsprawled on the yellow earth. In the blue moonlight a faint dust haze rose from the place where he lay motionless.

Leisurely Rio Jack returned his gun to leather and stepped into the sorrel's saddle. Unhurriedly he turned the animal's head and jogged away, recalling as he did so that nonchalant manner in which Nita earlier that evening had delivered him from Silvas's jail.

He did not go far, however. Not farther than the first dense mass of drifting shadows. There he turned the sorrel round and sat calmly watching the scene behind. A faint grin curled his lips as he perceived two men step hastily from the rear doorway of the squat adobe and lean above the peon he had felled. The grin widened and became sardonic as he watched them help the fellow to his feet, and heard the angry sound of guttural oaths.

When the three disappeared inside the building he found time to reflect upon the folly of his ways. Had he put a bullet through that peon, all might now be well. But in permitting the man to live he had placed an obstacle in the path of Nita's escape. That Villa would be wildly angry when he heard the fellow's tale, there could be no room for doubt.

What form would the general's wrath be likely to assume? he wondered. Would he order men on an instant search for the man he had just released? Or would his brutal rage be directed towards the girl he believed a spy?

He found tobacco and brown papers in the pocket of his scarlet shirt. Leisurely he rolled himself a smoke, struck a guarded match and lighted it behind cupped hands. He inhaled deeply while his mind worked feverishly to evolve some plan by which he could snatch the girl from her predicament.

But the trouble was that here was a situation in which bullets were powerless to effect a rescue. No matter how fast and true the thumbing hands of Rio Jack, Pancho Villa would win out by sheer weight of numbers. For once he was forced to admit there lay no hope of success in the bullet route.

With guns barred, what remained?

For long moments Rio Jack sat motionless in his saddle, his cigarette glowing red against the wavering mass of shadow. In the final reckoning one fact alone emerged. Nothing could be counted certain where Villa took a part. Once again he must thrust his head in the lion's mouth, and all because he had allowed convention to override his reason—because he had permitted that peon to live and carry tales!

His cigarette spun to the sand in a glowing arc, sent out a burst of sparks and died. Slowly he sent the sorrel across the moonlit open and back to the rear of the Limping Crow. With grim lips he swung from the saddle and, grounding his mount's reins, strode down the narrow passage towards the gambling rooms and the door-lined corridor beyond.

With a primitive barbarian of Villa's type, there was no use in formulating plans. He must act and improvise as emergencies arose. There was no other way.

As he passed through the gaming rooms he saw no indications of excitement or nervous tension that could not be accounted for by the reckless play indulged in by their occupants. Plainly a shooting scrape was no phenomenon at the Limping Crow.

But as he reached the door-lined corridor he saw a group of gesticulating soldiers arguing excitedly before the door of Villa's chamber. At sight of him their talk broke off with an

114

abruptness that was sinister. Five pairs of eyes regarded him with open hostility.

'*Buenas noches, amigos,*' he hailed.

'A fine night for a hanging!' growled a burly, dark-faced hombre in surly Spanish. 'Have you come back to feel the rope?'

Rio Jack chuckled easily. 'Tell Villa Rio Jack is here and desires a moment of his time.'

The man scowled but disappeared inside the room. In a moment he was back.

'The General waits.'

'*Gracias,*' drawled Rio Jack, and strode within the room. The soldier closed the door.

The staff officers were gone. There were three men only in the room beside himself. Fierro, the peon, and Villa—the latter, with legs dangling, sat on the table's edge, a cigarro between his strong white teeth, his lips half parted in that set smile which accompanied his attacks of anger.

'Because of you, my friend, I have not yet gone to bed and already the night is half gone. This fellow,' Villa stabbed a finger at the frightened peon, 'tells me you shot Garcia Escobar. Well, now I'm telling you, if this is true I have a hell of a good notion to hang you up for an example, papers or no papers.'

'You're the general,' Rio Jack's bronzed face was a lamplit mask. 'But if you think I was goin' to let that mozo pull a rod on me without squaring his account, you're dreaming.'

'Why should he pull a gun on you?'

115

'Ask me somethin' easy.'

'I will,' said Villa grimly. 'Why did you strike this fellow with your pistol?'

Rio Jack grinned. 'I guess I was kind of excited. I'm right sudden when I get excited.'

Villa expelled a cloud of smoke through his nostrils, his set smile never changing by a fraction. 'Listen, friend. I have an idea if I let you keep those pistols much longer you will ruin half my army. You get excited too often. You would have been a fine man for the Convention at Aguascalientes [*The Convention, after appointing Villa Commander-in-Chief of the army, had gone over to Carranga, in his estimation, and left him holding the sack.*] You could have showed those swine a thing or two.'

Suddenly he leaned forward. 'Why have you returned so soon? Did you get those ~~goddam~~ papers?'

'Not yet. They wouldn't let me off the bridge at the American side.'

'No?' Villa's eyes began to blaze. 'That is rather strange, don't you think?'

'They said they had heard you were in Sarizal and that no one should be permitted to cross until you left.'

'*Sangre de Dios!*' Villa exploded. 'Does all the world know I am at this pig-sty?'

Rio Jack grinned. 'I told you before that you were an important man. I came back to see if you want me to try the river.'

116

'Could you swim it with your arms and feet lashed?'

'Not very quick, I reckon.'

'Perhaps we shall see,' said Villa ominously, and flicked the ash from his cigarro. 'Now I will tell you why you shot Garcia Escobar. Two nights ago he was chasing this Guzman wench. She went up that placed called Satan's Toe. When he and his men would have followed, you shot at them from the top of the trail. Half an hour ago when you met him at the rear entrance of this place you shot him because you thought he would tell me this.'

It did not take any special insight on the part of Rio Jack to make him realize that he had walked into a trap. Nor did he have to be told that now the trap was about to spring. Yet his hard-bitten features reflected no emotion at Villa's correct diagnosis of the situation. For a moment he stood silent, then a faint grin tugged at his wide lips.

'That's God's truth and no mistake,' he said.

'What! You admit it, eh?' Villa's boiling anger nearly vanished in his astonishment.

'Why not?' countered Rio Jack. 'It's true enough. I shot Escobar because I was afraid he would tell you I was the man that balked him at Satan's Toe. But it is also true that he was draggin' at his gun when I killed him. I did not want him carrying tales to you because I figured you'd prob'bly grab the wrong impression.'

117

'What is this vast multitude of words? Speak plain, friend.'

'It's like this,' said Rio Jack. 'I took those papers from Miss Guzman at Satan's Toe, two nights ago. But if Escobar had told his tale, you would not have hesitated to order me shot on sight. I ain't hankerin' to be killed by your men when I'm workin' like hell to help you out.'

'That don't tell me why you stopped Escobar and his *ladrones* at Satan's Toe.'

'Isn't it obvious? I thought they were plain robbers. I knew the girl had those papers because I saw her take 'em from Ablon at the point of a gun. I was too far off to interfere. But I trailed her, saw she was headin' for that red rock hummock, an' got there first. Like I figured, the girl came. And after her came Escobar's bandits. I didn't want her to get away with them papers, an' I didn't want them outlaws to get 'em either. I fought them off, thinkin' it was the only way to make sure the papers would finally reach your hands.'

Villa looked undecided. Plainly he was suspicious. Yet equally plain was the fact that he wanted to believe Rio Jack's ingenious yarn. He needed fighting men, and Rio Jack's fame had travelled far.

As he watched the tawny general, it seemed to Rio Jack that he might just as well never have rediscovered Nevada Ablon for all the good it was apt to do him now. His pursuit of the lanky outlaw had brought him into a complex tangle of cross-purposes that seemed very likely to get the best of him and rid the Nevadan of his Nemesis for all time.

Whatever direction Villa's cogitations might have taken finally, he was never to know. For Fierro abruptly cut in upon them with a sardonic smile.

'A fine string of lies this hombre weaves, Chief.'

'You think so, pal?' Villa's clouding vision swung sharply to Rio Jack. 'Where have you hidden these papers of mine?'

'In the shack on Satan's Toe—Ablon's old hide-out,' he answered without hesitation. He knew that he must give Villa no further cause for suspicion or his life would be instant forfeit, considering the general's present state of mind.

'Describe the cache so one of my men can find it.'

'The papers are under the floor of the main room. The fourth board from the door works on a spring. When you step on the end nearest the wall, after moving the table, the other end lifts. Your man will find a narrow cavity underneath and in it your papers.' He paused, then added seriously:

'When I put them there the seals were still unbroken. If they are tampered with when you get them back it will be cause your messenger's curiosity got the better of his caution.'

There was danger in that addition as Rio Jack well knew. But although it would cause

119

Villa to suspect that he had already examined the contents of the elusive documents (which in fact he had never seen or even heard about until to-night), it would also provide the general with seemingly incontrovertible proof that the papers were actually where Rio Jack said they were.

Rio Jack's reasoning was proved accurate when Villa said to Fierro:

'Give Corva directions and tell him to swim the river if they will not let him cross the bridge. Tell him that one way or another I shall expect him back with those documents by nine to-morrow morning. It is after twelve now. He'd better fan some dust.'

When Fierro and the peon had gone, Villa turned to Rio Jack. As he spoke, the short ends of his tawny moustache threw moving shadows on his grinning lips.

'I'm telling you, friend; forty of my cavalrymen are hanging around with loaded guns and a desire to shoot. You won't leave this place without my permission, an' you won't get my permission until I see the colour of them papers. *Sabe?*'

'I'm free, white an' over twenty-one,' drawled Rio coldly.

'All right, you heard me; you try leaving and I'll lay you out cold.'

CHAPTER ELEVEN

BALKED

'That's a fine way to talk to a gent that's tryin' to help you.'

Villa's robust khaki-clad figure swung from the table. 'Never mind, friend. Time wasn't made to be lost in fool talk. If all you have said is true you will find Francisco Villa your best friend. But if Fierro was right and you've been telling me a pile of ▓▓▓▓dam lies, I'll hang you as soon as Corva proves it. Now get the hell out of here. I'm goin' to bed.'

When Rio Jack found himself in the corridor outside, he found its length deserted save for a pair of sentries who grinned when they saw him.

'How goes it, *amigo?*'

'We-ll,' Rio Jack observed, 'the rope's still several hours away. How far am I allowed to roam?'

'Not outside the hacienda—unless you feel a craving for hot lead.'

Humming a soft tune Rio Jack sauntered down the corridor towards the gambling rooms, the rhythmic ring of his spurs like silver chimes. The only exits from this place, as he had already discerned, were the front and rear doors. All the windows were heavily barred.

Still, things might be worse, he mused. After all, he still had the consolation of wearing his guns. With them and the handful of hours that must pass before Corva could return, much might yet be accomplished. He must keep his eyes peeled for Opportunity.

What bothered him mostly at the moment were the probable thoughts concerning him that were being entertained by Nita. She must consider him a blackguard of the widest stripe. How could she feel otherwise after he had so palpably cut loose of her? Certainly recent events—and events mainly engineered by himself—had painted him in muddy colours. How could any girl think well of a man who, to all intents and purposes, had saved his neck at the expense of hers?

It was a bitter thought for him to feel that she must be considering him as one of the deepest dyed villains afoot. For Rio Jack felt strongly drawn to her; desired above everything to appear well in her eyes. Never had he met a braver, more efficient girl, nor one more lovable than she, he told himself. She was the epitome of all things desirable.

He could visualize her now as he had first seen her that night on Satan's Toe with her blue-black hair agleam in the candle-light, her red lips parted in surprise, her lovely eyes deep pools of golden brown. He could see again the golden tan of her throat curving softly to the open collar of her woollen shirt, the rounded

122

contours of her breasts and the slim lithe waist beneath.

Her beauty was vital. About her there was an air of rugged honesty that he had seldom found in the women he had known. The sweet oval of her face and the spirited poise of her clean-limbed body attracted him mightily; just thinking of her brought a dull pounding to his heart and made the hot blood pulse more rapidly through his veins.

To realize what a beast she must be thinking him when every single thing he had done since entering the Limping Crow had been designed to extricate her from her difficulties, was bitter hard, he reflected, gloomily.

Entering the gaming rooms his eyes roved round with keen alertness. He tried to dismiss her from his mind and concentrate on finding some way of getting them clear of their unenviable situation.

If he had plenty of money in his pockets he might be able to do some advantageous bribing among the guard, he thought. But, unfortunately, he had not even a peso for the purpose.

He thought of using his guns to emulate El Buitre's stunt in the Singing Stopper; to hold up one of the gambling rooms and levy tax. But with a disgusted grunt he dismissed the notion as absurd. Even if he met with no interference from the patrons, it was a certainty that Villa's soldiers would shoot him down before he could take six steps. They fairly saturated the place. Everywhere he turned he could see their gleaming cartridge belts and ready rifles, their big hats and dark faces.

If somehow he could get the drop on Fierro, he mused, he might be able to force the fellow to pass them out. But as an obstacle to that notion was the fact that three or four alert troopers were constantly at the general's heels. And to risk pulling a gun on Fierro under such circumstances would be sheer suicide.

Presently he saw the sinister general take a seat at one of the gambling tables in a corner where a blank wall was at his back. The troopers lounged on either side as Fierro prepared to test his luck.

Rio thought, 'Now's the time if ever!' and proceeded to put in action a plan he had just evolved. It was pretty desperate, but it was just possible it might succeed.

Hurrying away from the distant room in which Fierro was apparently engrossed with his gambling Rio Jack made his way towards the door-lined corridor off which opened the girl's temporary prison. The guards looked up indifferently as he approached.

Assuming an air of great assurance, he said to the sentry before the door to Nita's room: 'General Fierro orders you to fetch the prisoner an' follow me,' and he tapped a pocket into which he had folded a bit of newspaper as though it contained written orders.

The sentry, a burly fellow with a swarthy face and a cast in one eye, looked him over as though amused. 'Yeah?'

'Yeah!' he snapped with angry emphasis. 'Don't you understand your own language?'

'I understand, *señor*, but my orders were to stay here until I was relieved by General Fierro himself.'

Rio Jack's spirits dropped several degrees. If this were so, it meant that the wily Fierro had something up his sleeve regarding the girl; something which Villa patently knew nothing about. He recalled the sinister tale of how Fierro with his own hand had shot three hundred prisoners in lots of ten as his soldiers forced them to bolt across a long open space towards a six-foot adobe wall. It was understood that any who got over the wall were free to go. The first ten Fierro had greeted with these encouraging words, 'Come on, boys; I'm only going to shoot, and I'm a bad shot.' Of the three hundred prisoners but one man cleared the wall and got away.

And now this fiendish hound had ordered the sentry to stay by the girl's door until he personally came to relieve him! It was a thought to start cold chills.

Rio Jack's jaw snapped forward and his cold grey eyes stared the sentry down. 'I know all that,' his voice was testy, irritable. 'But things have changed. Do you know who I am?'

'No, Chief. I have heard—'

'Never mind what you've heard. A pack of lies, no doubt. I am General Villa's new chief of staff.' He slapped his holstered guns with suggestive palms.

Both sentries were now eyeing him with close attention. No doubt they were recalling their pleasantries of a while back and wondering if they were to be punished for their witticisms. The man to whom he had addressed himself swallowed nervously and rubbed a dry lower lip with his left hand.

'You don't say so, General!'

'Yes. And let me tell you it will go mighty hard with any fool who ignores my orders. Now fetch the Señorita Guzman instantly and follow me.'

Still the man paused undecided. Rio Jack could almost read the workings of his sluggish mind. He was debating no doubt the advisability of disobeying Fierro's orders in favour of the stranger's. For a number of moments the matter seemed to hang in the balance. Then Fierro's sinister reputation appeared to win.

'Will you pardon me, General, if I go to seek advice about this?'

'Advice!' blustered Rio Jack, attempting to override the other's caution. 'I can give you some advice, fellow! I advise you to do as I say pronto unless you desire to face a firing squad for disobedience!'

126

'But, General!' protested the sentry, with excited gestures. 'No matter which of you I obey, I must disobey the other!'

'A pretty dilemma,' agreed Rio Jack, with curling lip. 'Make up your mind quick fellow. I am getting impatient.'

With a despairing glance at his comrade, the sentry produced a key and thrust it in the door. For a moment Rio Jack's spirits abounded high, then fell with a thud as the nearing clatter of running boots was heard and a hatless soldier came dashing down the corridor with wild eyes.

'Quick!' the newcomer gasped. '*Quick! Arouse the Chief!*'

Rio Jack grabbed him by the shoulders and shook him violently. 'What's up? You should know the General's not to be disturbed when he is sleeping. Talk fast, hombre!'

The panting soldier swore incoherently. 'Carranza's men! General Nafarrate! The town is being surrounded!'

Startled fright stamped the faces of the sentries. Rio Jack searched the soldier's sweating features probingly. 'If this is some hoax—' he began, when the messenger cut in frenziedly:

'It is not! I swear it, General! Four detachments of cavalry! I was posted on the hill and saw them with my eyes! It is that cursed dog of a Nafarrate!'

Rio Jack swung round on the gaping

sentries. 'Quick! Give me that key,' he grabbed it from the fellow's unresisting hand. Go warn the men—both of you! *Hurry!*'

'Follow me!' he snapped to the hatless Mercury and, slipping the key in his pocket, he strode to Villa's door and pounded heavily. This, he was thinking though it might spoil their immediate chance of escape, certainly offered him an opportunity of putting himself in solid with the irate Pancho. An opportunity too good to miss!

As he hammered again, making the door rattle with his clamour, a thunderous sound of rageful oaths broke out within the room. Abruptly the door was flung open and Rio Jack found himself staring into the glaring muzzle of Villa's enormous pistol.

'What the hell do you mean by waking me up this way?' growled the general murderously, running his left hand through the tangled mass of tawny hair that hung upon his forehead. 'By God—'

'Stow it, Pancho,' Rio Jack cut in, only by the utmost effort of will holding his voice to a low, calm drawl. 'This man,' he pulled the reluctant soldier forward, 'just arrived. He says General Nafarrate with four detachments of cavalry is manoeuvring to surround the town.'

'He does! He is!' Villa swore with reckless abandon. 'The dirty son of a bitch! Some day that dirty coyote will learn that I ain't no safe man to fool with!' He swung his restless tiger

128

gaze upon the frightened soldier. 'You go spread the alarm and be quick about it.'

'I've already taken care of that, General,' Rio Jack cut in.

'Who the hell told you to give orders around this place?'

'Didn't you make me a colonel?'

Villa glared, then suddenly grinned. 'That's right, friend. Well, you'll see some action tonight. We leave for my camp in ten minutes. Order the men to horse. I'll join them out back. Send Fierro to me right away,' and, having delivered these commands in a rapid voice, he swung back into the room.

Rio Jack grabbed the hatless soldier and sent him running down the corridor with a hasty shove. 'Carry out the General's orders! Don't stand around with your mouth open. Get a move on!'

When the man was out of sight, he produced the key he had taken from the sentry and swiftly unlocked the door to the girl's room. 'Nita!' he whispered hoarsely.

No answer came from the darkened chamber.

'Nita!' his voice was urgent.

'What do you want?'

'Did you hear that conversation?'

'Yes,' came the girl's uncompromising tone.

'Well, hurry out of there then. We've got to move fast if we're going to get out of this. May be the only chance we'll get. There's no one in

129

sight right now.'

'Then I guess I'll wait until there is!'

Rio Jack managed to stifle his exasperated groan. Was this to be the reward for all the risk he had taken on her behalf? Not that he wanted any reward, but he certainly did not wish to remain within Villa's reach any longer than necessary.

'Don't you want to get away?'

'Not with you.'

He could have spanked her for her obstinacy. Now that the first real chance had opened for a getaway this girl, through spite at his earlier actions which she plainly misinterpreted, refused to budge an inch. He could see but one way to handle the situation—force.

With this thought in mind he strode within the darkened room.

'Don't be a fool! I'm tryin' all I know how to help you out of this mess—'

'You're a damned liar!' she lashed back, and her whispering voice seemed all the more fierce for its very softness.

He winced at the appellation. Certainly he had lied a-plenty; there was no getting around that. But he would not tell her that all his lies had been designed to smooth the way for her escape. His pride forbade him doing that.

He searched his pockets hurriedly for a match, finally finding one in the leather band about his hat. Its sharp yellow light, as it flooded the room, showed him a candle stuck in a bottle-neck. He lit it, swiftly.

He eyed her a moment with calculating gaze. In her present mood he thought her more beautiful than ever. She stood against the far wall, chin high. In the slumbering pools of her golden eyes he read a look of mingled resentment and defiance.

The red lips curled. 'Well?'

'Listen. I'm tryin' to get you out of this mess. I ain't sure what it's all about an' I don't give a damn. But I can't help you much if you won't trail your luck with mine.'

'I can do without the sort of help you're giving me. No real man,' her tones were flat with contempt, 'would ever act the way you've done—would ever save himself at the expense of a helpless girl! Not that I'm helpless. It's the principle of the thing. "I knew she was a Carranza spy,"' she mimicked with curling lips. 'As though you couldn't have helped me without saying that!'

He could have explained that he had hoped by accusing her to place himself more solidly with Villa, so that later he might have a better chance, as he had right now, of getting her clear.

But instead he strode forward abruptly, took her bare arm in his firm, hard fingers. He cursed softly as he realized that his hands shook a little at contact with her flesh.

'Look at me,' he ordered grimly. 'Do I look

131

the sort that would shield himself behind a woman without damn good reason?'

'Your dramatics are wasted, Mister Golden.' she stared straight ahead, and there were little flames in her golden eyes. Her mouth, usually so red and provocative, was a white, straight line of unyielding defiance.

His grip tightened. 'Good Lord, girl! Don't be a fool! We've got to hurry or we're trapped!'

'Then let's be trapped,' she said, and smiled coldly.

He shook her then, angrily, fiercely, attempting to break her stubborn resistance.

The smile left her lips. They curled back showing her even teeth gleaming in the candlelight. Her eyes blazed with fury. 'Damn you! Get your hands off me!'

From without came the sound of mounting men; the jingle of spur chains and the creak of saddle leather.

With all haste Rio Jack picked her up bodily and started for the door. She writhed and squirmed and kicked in silent resistance. He could feel her breasts against him, throbbing with the fury of her struggles. Her fists hammered against his face. But he only laughed and bore her through the door. In the corridor he came face to face with Villa, hurrying to join his men.

'Good work, friend,' the general chuckled. 'I see you have a way with women. Bring the little hellcat with you. We leave immediately,' and down the hall he strode, Rio Jack following with the still-struggling girl, whose face had crimsoned at Villa's words.

'How I hate you!' she panted, her burning cheeks within three inches of his own. 'Some day you will pay dear for this, I swear it!'

'Save your threats for those who care,' he jeered, angry that her obstinacy had balked them of escape. 'If you'd used a little of that wild energy to think things out, we'd been away from her now. As it is, we've got to go with Villa.'

CHAPTER TWELVE

A BIT OF BUSINESS

In the blue silver of the waning night Rio Jack, carrying his momentarily-passive burden, beheld as he strode from the rear door of the Limping Crow a dark mass of mounted men. The scouting party that had accompanied Villa to Sarizal was ready to ride. The general himself was in the saddle and beside him on a dappled grey sat the saturnine Fiero.

Rio Jack strode to the long-legged sorrel gelding being held for him by a steeple-hatted soldier. He swung the girl to the saddle and swung up behind her. 'All ready, Chief.'

The dark mass of horsemen got in motion. With Villa and Fierro leading, Rio Jack swung in behind, and back of him the others strung out in a long double line, the moonlight glistening on their rifle-barrels and their belts of gleaming shells.

Villa led southwest, passing back orders that there be no talking nor smoking on penalty of death.

It was plain to Rio Jack that the Chief was anxious to avoid a skirmish and guessed that the cause lay in the superior number of Nafarrate's force. He had often heard of Villa, with a mere handful of men, attacking much larger numbers than those at present commanded by Carranza's henchman. Perhaps some deep strategy lay behind his present flight.

Be that as it may, Villa was undoubtedly desirous of fleeing in the present instance without the firing of a shot. The long line streamed into the deep shadow of a stand of lodgepole and aspen and threaded its way with caution. Only the creaking of saddle leather and the occasional tinkle of spur chains, together with the soft thud of horses' hoofs, disturbed the vast silence of the night.

In fifteen minutes they were out of the sheltering shadows of the trees and were loping across the glaring white waste of a moonlit desert.

A breath of cooler air fanned the faces of the silent horsemen, welcome after the heat of the woods they had left behind. Before them stretched a sea of endless sand, shot here and there with the dagger forms of cactus.

The mystery of the open desert lay upon them.

From the tops of numerous rises Rio Jack caught fleeting glimpses of the vast country through which they were riding. A mighty world of silence, space and desolation that seemed majestic in its solemn beauty. The silver of the sliding moon and the ochre of the barren wastes lent softening touches to a country he knew was harsh by light of day.

But the nearness of Nita swiftly drew his thoughts from abstract beauty. She leaned forward in her saddle as she rode, keeping as far away from him as the demands of the situation permitted. Yet even so, the fragrance of her blue-black hair was in his nostrils and the rhythmic roll of her shoulders to the motion of the horse was pleasant in his eyes.

What a girl! he thought, and winced as he recalled her opinion of him.

The stars blinking down from the azure heavens looked soft as sleepy mockers, and seemed but a rope's throw away. Yet even so they were no further off than was the girl who sat before him, he reflected sombrely. Though close in flesh, he well knew what a vast chasm separated them in spirit.

For some time thereafter he pondered on the futility of existence, and only roused when the dark mass of huddled buildings in the distance

135

marked the site of a small town.

Abruptly Villa's hand flung up and the column halted. Twisting about in his saddle the general raised his voice.

'We're going to stop in that town. It will be dawn by the time we get there. We'll stop till noon to rest our horses. Kindly see that the privacy of those people's homes is not disturbed. *Sabe?*'

At the guttural response, Villa turned his back and the column loped on.

From the southward a lobo's deep howl came wailing across the winds. In the west the stars and moon began to dim. Chill daybreak was drawing near as they approached the tiny town and the farflung waste of sand about it lay grey and lifeless. A great red streak showed in the eastern sky where the sun was preparing to get out of bed. It began to grow light. The red streak widened, glowed swiftly crimson, became shot with gold.

Suddenly the sun poked its smiling face above the desert's rim and flung it's warming rays across the night-chilled sand, glanced scintillating off the polished tubes of the riders' rifles and turned the nearing adobe walls of the houses golden, in their crevices creating cobalt shadows.

The long main street was deserted as they swept up and into its northern end.

Dismounting, the riders stripped the gear from their weary horses and turned them into

the public corral. Villa dispatched two of h[...]
men to secure the use of a large adobe dwelling
in the centre of town. They returned a short
time later with its expostulating owner.

'But where will I go if you take over my
house?' the man wailed.

'You can go to hell, hombre, for all of me,'
said Villa. 'but your house is needed for the
Cause. If you and your family are not out of it
in ten minutes I will have my soldiers move you
out. *Vamose!*'

'But, General! I have a daughter—'

'What? A virgin?' Villa winked at Fierro.
Fierro's handsome face broke into a grin.

The frightened man wrung his hands.
'*Sangre de Dios, General!* Is this justice?'

'Did that son of a bitch Ullalio give me
justice? Surely you cannot consider yourself
better than me who work my hands to the bone
and place my neck in the shadow of the noose
all for love of my country? What have you done
for Mexico?'

The fellow hurriedly slunk away.

Villa looked after him and swore. Turning to
Rio Jack who stood close by with Nita, he
asked:

'Can you imagine that, friend? Talking to me
about justice! I bet he's never shot one single
bullet in defence of his country. Justice!' he
snorted, without waiting for an answer. 'If I
strung him up by the neck, he'd be getting the
kind of justice he deserves!'

137

'Do you think it will be safe stopping here?' began Rio Jack. 'Nafarrate—'

'That butcher! Pah! he would not have nerve enough to follow me here. My army is encamped not twenty miles away. That for Nafarrate,' said Villa, and snapped his fingers contemptuously.

Turning to Fierro, he said: 'Collect my staff officers and follow me to that fellow's house.' He beckoned Rio Jack. 'Bring that girl along.'

Without further word his robust, khaki-clad figure went swinging up the street. Rio Jack and the girl swung in behind. He caught her eyes upon him and whispered softly:

'First chance comes our way, we'll make a break and try to get to Nafarrate.'

She was still without boots and blood and dust were caked on her slender feet. He noticed that she limped a little and his heart went out to her. She had been through a lot in the last twelve hours, yet not a whimper had he heard.

'You must trust me, Nita,' he whispered earnestly. 'I know things look pretty black against me, an' I admit I told a pile of lies. But I thought I could fix it so I'd find a way to get you clear. Darn it, girl—if we're forced to go to Villa's camp I'm afraid we're done. All hell couldn't help you then!'

Her hands were tight-clenched. All during his monologue she had held her face straight ahead, never once looking at him, her chin defiant.

He was about to vent a muttered oath when he saw her lips move slightly. He bent nearer and heard the murmured words:

'All right. If you see a chance, I'll back your play.'

His heart bounded with exultation. In spite of her poor opinion of him, she had decided to give him a chance. He followed the general now with a lighter step. The world took on a rosier hue. Never, he thought, had the sun appeared so bright. It was rapidly getting hot, but he never noticed, so exhilarated was he to think that at last Nita, if not exactly trusting him, had at least agreed to back his play if he saw another chance to get her out of Villa's hands.

Her concession was born of necessity, of course. But that did not make it any the less sweet in the mind of Rio Jack.

The place Villa's two officers had picked out for his temporary headquarters was a great adobe building in the form of a square about an open patio or court. Its shuttered windows were deeply recessed against the heat in six foot walls. Gritty winds from off the desert had long since sanded its harsh corners until now it appeared as one with the sun-baked earth about it.

Cottonwoods reared their dusty foliage above it, rattling dryly in the hot wind as the morning sun rose higher Their swaying motion threw wavering cobalt shadows across its sun-drenched walls. Heat waves rose and fell above the dusty road.

The owner and his family and retainers were gone when Rio Jack and the girl, following the tawny general, arrived. The interior of the dwelling was cool in heady contrast to the simmering heat outside. Striding into the *sala* of the casa Villa turned to Rio Jack.

'Lock the girl in one of the rooms and put a sentry outside her door, friend. Then rejoin me here. We will eat together. I have something I want you to do. I'll tell you all about it as we eat.'

Rio Jack saluted.

* * *

When he returned to the *sala*, or main room of the house, he found Villa's staff assembled. Fierro, too, was there and cast a saturnine glance at him as he came in. They were all seated about a long table brought from another part of the house. The table, Rio Jack saw in some surprise, was laden with food. Villa had a way with him, he reflected grimly, wondering where the general had managed to get food so swiftly. He noted that they had saved him a place.

Taking the empty chair Rio Jack sat down and silently commenced his breakfast. He wanted to ask if the girl was going to be fed, but as the others were engrossed in a conversation

140

concerning military matters he deemed the question inadvisable. They would hardly starve the girl, he reasoned, no matter what ultimate fate they might be planning for her.

He noticed that Villa's repast was very frugal, confirming what he had heard of the general's habits. It consisted solely of a portion of baked sweet potato washed down with two glasses of milk.

When he had finished, Villa shoved back his chair.

'Colonel Oro,' he said to Rio Jack, 'I have some work for you. We are badly in need of supplies at my camp. Then, too, there is the matter of my men's wages to be taken care of. Frankly, we have not sufficient dinero for these purposes I am going to ask for aid—a loan of some sort—from a few of the prominent reactionaries [*The term given by Villa to the opposition forces.*] of this town.'

'How much money you figurin' to need?' questioned Rio Jack.

'A mere matter of twenty thousand *pesos*,' Villa said, and chuckled at the look of incredulity on the cowboy's face.

'You'll never get no twenty thousand out of this two-bit burg,' scoffed Rio Jack.

'That's where you're wrong, friend. I shall get every *centavo* of that amount.'

Villa ran the fingers of his left hand through the bushy mass of tawny hair that stood out above his forehead. 'Yes,' he said with slow relish, 'I shall get every bit of twenty thousand—perhaps more. Fierro, here, has a plan that's bound to click. It's been tried out more than once.'

After rummaging through several pockets he brought to light a scrap of paper which he reached across the table to Rio Jack. 'You take this paper,' he said, 'and round up all the fellows whose names are on here. Four of them—the four most influential men in this place. One has land. Another has land and a store. One of them even has cash. And that's a bad thing. Here are we who have risked our lives—our pure, unsullied lives—in the cause of democracy and we have not got the thinnest *centavo* to our name.'

Glancing round the table, as though for confirmation, Villa went on:

'These hombres were supporters of that dog of a Huerta. You gather them up and see that they report here immediately. Otherwise they will be shot for giving aid and comfort to the enemy.'

As the general talked, orderlies were constantly coming and going, their arms loaded with equipment and divers baggage.

'Take ten of my *dorados* and attend to this matter at once.'

Rio Jack saluted and left the table. He was not at all pleased at having been given this order as it would take him away from the vicinity of Nita for some time. He would have

142

preferred to have remained within earshot of the girl in case some unforeseen circumstance should demand instant action on his part. But there was no help for it; Villa had issued an order and it must be obeyed.

The *dorados*—or guilded men—of Villa's bodyguard were easily distinguished from the regular soldiers because of their uniforms being so resplendent with gold braid and other ornaments. In no time Rio Jack had collected ten of them and set about locating the four men from whom the general expected to make his 'loan.'

In the plaza he obtained the needed information but as he and the *dorados* tramped up and down the town, alarm spread rapidly. The citizens eyed him askance from the doorways and windows of their houses.

Three of the four men were found promptly, as everyone knew of them, their homes and places of business. As Villa had said, these men were the town's aristocrats. But the fourth man on the list took a deal of finding. Everyone was sure the general could have no need of him.

'Chico Urristra? Indeed! Certainly not Chico?'

'Yes, *Chico*,' Rio Jack said firmly. 'Is there no such person?'

'To be sure. But no one could mistake Chico for one of our leading citizens. He is but a cobbler, and a bad one, at that. Why, he is poorer than a dog, since even a dog has fleas.

Chico has nothing save scraps of rusty leather.'

Nevertheless, as his orders called for the apprehension of Chico Urristra, even though it seemed the general had made a mistake in placing his name on the list, Rio Jack and the *dorados* brought him to headquarters with the three legitimate aristocrats.

Villa received the four men with all ceremony. Indeed, he seemed to put himself out to be polite—an unusual thing with him. He stood behind the table with his campaign jacket buttoned to the throat, freshly shaven, his hat shoved not so far back on his tawny head as usual. Standing along the wall behind him were his staff officers. Fierro lounged nearby.

Rio Jack stood at attention while, for several minutes, Villa permitted the dragging silence to tighten up. The mechanical grin was on his lips as he began to speak.

'Gentlemen, I rejoice to see you, though I shall not clasp your hands because you four are cowardly traitors, disloyal citizens, flagrant enemies of your country and all its free institutions. As the Commander-in-Chief of the brave army of the revolution—'

'But, General!' Chico Urristra began when the general pulled him up short.

'Under no circumstances, gentlemen, am I to be interrupted!'

As though to make sure that there would be no further interpolation on the part of the four

144

townsmen, Rio Jack found the general looking at him sternly and saying:

'Colonel, make sure there are no more of these interruptions!'

Rio Jack saluted. 'Present *arms!*' he ordered the ten *dorados*, who did so with a fiercely threatening air.

The general then scanned the list which Rio Jack had returned to him.

'Which one of you is Chico Urristra?'

'Me, General,' replied the little cobbler.

'Hmm.' Villa frowned. 'Which is Don Cipriano Caldez?'

'I!' snapped a thin haughty voice.

'Well, well—glad to know you, friend.' The general glanced at the paper again as though to refresh his memory (which had never been known to need such treatment). 'And Ricardo Alvarez. Which of you is Don Ricardo?'

'Your obedient servant, General.'

'Well, I'm glad to hear it. We shall see—Yes, we shall certainly see. And you,' said Villa, turning to the ony man who had not spoken, 'must be Don Manuel Llorentes.'

'Right.'

'Now this is fine, gentlemen,' chuckled Villa, warming up for business. 'Now the matter on which I have called you here is urgent. The revolution—the triumph of Right over base Corruption—demands funds, as you may guess. Unfortunately, we find our coffers empty. In such an instance it is only fair that you—the classes and persons directly responsible for this deplorable state of affairs—should defray the expenses of a war for which you and your kind are alone responsible.

'My troops must be paid. We must have supplies. These soldiers whom you see about your town this morning, fought half the night with the cavalry of the reactionary general, Nafarrate. I need not say they were victorious. Their presence here this morning proves it. By their brave actions my faithful followers have driven off the horde who would have sacked this beautiful town. Therefore, it becomes my privilege to suggest that you gentlemen supply, with neither pretexts nor delays of any kind, the insignificant sum of twenty thousand *pesos*.

'I do not wish to seem unfair. So we will consider this not a punishment for aiding the enemies of Liberty, but as an obligatory loan for which each one of you will be given a receipt.

'There are but two stipulations I wish to impress upon you, gentlemen. These: that the amount assigned to each of you will not be altered by one *centavo*, and that the time allotted to produce it will not be extended by a second.'

It was obvious to Rio Jack and all others in the room at the conclusion of Villa's talk that all four of the townsmen were in a state of apprehension bordering close upon panic. The

146

veins in their foreheads were bulging, they kept swallowing as though some part of their breakfast had found lodging in their throats. Their fingers twisted nervously behind their backs. Only the little cobbler seemed to maintain a relative tranquillity.

After a slight pause Villa rumbled on:

'Chico Urristra, you are granted a period of two hours, beginning right now—7:15 a.m.—to supply the troops of the revolution with the sum of five thousand *pesos*. If this demand is not complied with inside the two hours you will be hanged promptly at 9:15 a.m.'

It seemed to Rio Jack that all breathing in the row of townsmen had become suspended. Their faces, scarlet a moment before, now turned deathly white. Chico made movements with his mouth but no sound issued. Fierro grinned sardonically.

The general went inexorably on:

'Don Cipriano Caldez, we grant you a period of three hours, beginning now, to supply us with the sum of six thousand *pesos*. If the money is not forthcoming by 10:20 a.m. you will be promptly hanged without further preliminaries.

'Don Ricardo Alvarez, we grant you an allotment of four hours to produce for us the sum of seven thousand *pesos*. If, in your country's interests, you have not complied with this demand by 11:22 a.m. you will be

147

hanged at that time without formalities of any kind.

'Don Manuel Llorentes, we give you five hours to procure for us the sum of eight thousand *pesos*. If at the hour of twelve twenty-five that sum in your name has not been paid into our treasury, we shall hang you, pausing only to be sure the clock is right.

'One more word, gentlemen, and I shall be through. While the gathering of these sums is being carried out by members of your families and friends, you may consider yourselves prisoners here at headquarters. Although given every chance to freely communicate with friends and relatives, you will be under the eyes of my *dorados* until the amounts are paid.'

Villa then gave orders to one of his staff officers to see that the prisoners were quartered under guard.

Chico Urristra finally found his voice.

'General—'

'You will waste your time, friend, trying to crawl out of this.'

'But, General! I have no money—I am very poor in every way. Poor in money, poor in friends and poor in relatives. It will be absolutely impossible for me to raise five hundred *pesos*, let alone five thousand. For that amount two years would be far too little time, I assure you. There is no need for a two-hour wait. Bring on your rope and hang me now.'

'My friend, you will be given two hours as I promised. Francisco Villa always keeps his word. If, at the end of that time, you have not procured the money, rest assured that you will hang.'

'A fine business!' Rio Jack muttered to himself as he left the room. Judging from what he had heard about town, Chico Urristra would be unable to scrape up even so few as five *pesos*—let alone such a sum as five thousand. Plainly the little cobbler was doomed.

Now, he decided, was a fine chance to visit Nita. If she had not received a breakfast he had determined to secure one for her without delay. Likewise boots and a hat. Perhaps he could find a woman or a doctor who would be able to do something for her feet, although in truth her feet were in little worse shape than his own, which hurt at every step.

'But, hell,' he growled. 'A man is supposed to stand such things as that an' grin. It's diff'rent with a girl. A woman's more tender in her feelin's than a man.'

He felt sorry for the four townsmen who were doomed to beggar themselves or hang. But after all, he reasoned, it was none of his business and there was nothing he could do about it even if he wanted to. 'Might speak to the general about Chico, anyway,' he thought, and turned back.

But Villa only laughed. 'You're new to this

149

business,' he chuckled. 'These fellows would fool you easy, friend. But it takes a smart man to fool Pancho Villa. You mark my words, of the four men we have imprisoned here, the most valuable one of all for us is this same Chico Urristra. You wait and see.'

Shaking his head, Rio Jack went out and once again headed for the room in which the girl was being held. As he strode through the patio, he saw and heard a group of soldiers singing Villa's favourite song. A *dorado* was accompanying them on a guitar:

'All the maidens are of pure gold;
All the married girls are silver;
All the widows are of copper,
And old women merely tin.

All the girls up at Las Vegas
Are most awful tall and skinny,
But they're worse for plaintive pleading
Than the souls in Purgatory.

All the girls here in the city
Don't know how to give you kisses,
While the ones from Albuquerque
Stretch their necks to avoid misses.

La Cucaracha, La Cucaracha,
Doesn't want to travel on
Because she hasn't,
Oh no, she hasn't,

150

Marihuana for to smoke.'

But as he stopped beside a door before which the sentry who had guarded the girl's door at the Limping Crow was standing, it was not of the music or the song that Rio Jack was thinking. It was of Nevada Ablon, the man he had pursued up and down the border for four long, dusty years. It seemed to him now that unless he got away from Villa soon he would never live to catch the man.

CHAPTER THIRTEEN

WHEN THE DEVIL LAUGHED

Nita regarded him with grave eyes as he stepped inside the room. She was sitting on a little bed beside the window and the sunlight, seeping in between the bars, illumined her oval face that was framed by the lovely mass of her long dark hair.

Several buttons, he noticed, were missing from her woollen shirt, no doubt lost in the river crossing the night before. Because of their lack her shirt seemed open further down than it had formerly been. He could see the white valley of flesh between her breasts and the sight fascinated him. But he roused himself and looked away as he caught the angry blush that

151

was stealing across her drawn features.

But though there were dark circles of fatigue beneath her golden eyes, and tiny lines about her lips, he thought that never had he seen her so beautiful as she appeared to him now. Just to look at her made his heart pound faster and caused him to feel a bit giddy as though from staring down a mighty precipice.

'When are we going to leave here?' she asked abruptly.

'Well, not till around one o'clock, anyway. The general is making some loans and won't leave till the deals are finished. It may take a little time. He's allowing five hours. Between you an' me, I reckon the only reason we stopped here at all was to fix up them loans.'

'That isn't what I mean,' she said. 'I want to know when we are leaving—you and I?'

'Oh. That's kind of hard to tell. I'm watchin' for a break. But I doubt if we'll get one till after this business is finished. Villa's got men posted all around to make sure none of the prisoners escape. But first chance I see I'll sure make a try. Have you had any breakfast?'

She nodded. 'Yes, a peon brought me in something. But I'm too worried to enjoy eating. I want to get away from here. I want to get away from here quick.'

'Well, I'll sure do my best to oblige,' he said, and, thinking of nothing further to discuss that was important enough to risk being discovered in her room by Villa or Fierro, took his

152

departure.

In the patio the soldiers were still singing:

'One thing makes me laugh most hearty—
Pancho Villa with no shirt on
Now the Carranzistas beat it
Because Villa's men are coming.

La Cucaracha, La Cucaracha,
Doesn't want to travel on
Because she hasn't,
Oh no, she hasn't,
Marihuana for to smoke.'

As Rio Jack stepped once again into the *sala* where Villa had established his headquarters, the tawny general was preaching a moral doctrine to his staff.

'You must never,' he said, 'do violence to women. Lead them all to the altar; you know these church marriages don't mean a thing. That way you don't have to lose your good time and you don't make them unhappy. Why, look at me: I've got my legal wife that I married before the Justice of the Peace, but I've got others that are legitimate too in the sight of God, or of the law that means most to them, which is the same thing. That way they're not ashamed or embarrassed, because whatever slip or sin there may have been is mine. What could be better than an easy conscience and a nice friendly understanding with the women you take a notion to? Don't pay any attention if the priest objects or grumbles; just threaten to put a bullet through him and you'll see how he comes round.' [*Quoted from page 310 of Martin Luis Guzman's* The Eagle and the Serpent.]

Noticing Rio Jack, the general said:

'There is but an hour left for Chico Urristra to dwell on *terra firma*. He has secured not one *centavo* as yet. And it begins to look as though he does not mean to. You must hurry and get things ready for his hanging. We will use one of those tall cottonwoods in the yard for a gallows, friend. Have a couple of the men climb up and put a nice stout rope on the strongest branch. A rope with a slip-noose at the end. No ordinary knot now. I want this thing done right. We must have a hangman's knot. You see to it, friend.'

As Rio Jack strode into the patio to give the general's order, he racked his brain to find some way out of the mess for poor Chico. It seemed a shame to hang the little cobbler when it would have been obvious to a blind man that he had neither money nor the means of securing any.

But though his heart rebelled at the fate Villa was planning for the unfortunate man, he could see no way of successful intervention. It would do no good to remonstrate with Villa. His mind was made up. Only misfortune could come to the man who sought to change it, and Rio Jack dared not further risk his already

154

precarious standing with the general. For well he realized that he was Nita's only hope. Her very fact in finally agreeing to back any play he saw fit to make was definite proof that she regarded him as her last resort.

He passed on the general's orders.

At nine o'clock all was ready. At five after nine Villa sent to ask if Chico was ready to hand over his share of the loan. He answered that he was ready enough, but that he did not have the money and saw no slightest hope of getting it. With a grin, Villa turned the whole affair over to General Fierro.

Fierro ordered a squad of soldiers to bring the prisoners out beneath the cottonwood that had been made ready for a gallows. He then said to Rio Jack:

'Order every officer in the casa to report outside at once.'

When Rio Jack got to the yard, deep silence greeted him. Several feet to one side of the tall cottonwood the rich men sentenced to the loan or sudden death stood in a motionless line. There was terror on their faces. In double column at the right stood the twenty soldiers. To the left there was a semi-circle composed of the officers Rio Jack had summoned. In the order of their rank they stood grouped about Fierro. Rio Jack took his place among them. Villa, he noticed, was not present.

A sergeant joined the soldiers. A corporal left the ranks and strode to a chair that had been placed in line with the dangling noose beneath the tree.

The time was nine-thirteen. Rio Jack saw that the four prisoners were deathly pale. Chico, he thought, seemed the calmest of them all. When Rio Jack looked at him he was licking his dry lips with a furtive tongue. Perhaps even yet he thought the business just a farce to scare him.

Fierro took from his pocket the fatal list. In a deep voice he said:

'Chico Urristra.'

'Yes, sir.'

'Are you going to obey General Villa's orders?'

'Like I told him, General, I would be only too glad to do so, but I haven't any money.'

'Very well. I will show you the way we treat such men as you. Sergeant! See that the fellows' hands are tied and stand him on that chair!'

When the order was fulfilled, Fierro snapped:

'Fix that noose about his neck, corporal.'

And the soldier did so, the sergeant stepped back to his double line of men.

'Present *arms*!'

Rio Jack saw that the legs of the other three prisoners were shaking and that their terror-filled eyes were nearly popping from their heads. Yet, as though they dared not look away, they were following Chico's every movement and everything that was being done to him.

A sombre smile curled Fierro's thin lips. 'Chico Urristra, it is now nine-fifteen. Your allotted time is up. Will you hand over the money? Yes or no?'

Chico did not answer.

'All right, corporal!' Fierro snapped. 'Yank that chair away!'

The soldier made haste to obey his order. The unlucky cobbler was left dangling from the rope. The noose jerked tight. Urristra's legs threshed the air and a ghastly expression came over his twisted face.

The three surviving townsmen screamed and hastily covered their eyes. Even the officers turned their heads away. One or two of them could not repress a shudder.

Rio Jack felt violently sick.

But Fierro eyed the dangling shape with a complacent smile.

Needless to say, the object lesson provided by Urristra's fate caused the three remaining prisoners to pay up promptly. In a short time Villa announced that they would soon be on their way to his camp at the railhead. Rio Jack went off to have a final word with Nita before saddling up.

'Is there nothing you can do to get me away?' demanded Nita, nervously.

'Well, I've worked up a plan,' Rio Jack admitted, 'but I ain't puttin' a lot of hope into it. The devil of it is that with an impulsive hombre like Pancho, a fellow can't figure very

157

close on anything. There's no tellin' which way he'll jump. Logic don't mean a thing to him.'

'Well, do something quick,' she spoke impatiently.

Plainly, thought Rio Jack, her predicament was beginning to get on her nerves. Her face was pale and her hands kept twisting nervously where they lay in her lap. Her blue-black hair was tousled as though she had been running her hand through it in her distress.

'I'll do my best,' he promised. 'Villa's aimin' to break camp here in a few minutes. Before he leaves we'll know enough whether or not this scheme of mine is goin' to work. Keep a stiff upper lip,' he smiled encouragingly as he went out.

In the patio the soldiers were still singing, though now the song being rendered was slightly different:

'If Adelita would take me for a husband,
If Adelita would only be my wife,
I would buy her a costume of satin
And I'd give her a taste of barracks life.

Now the trumpet of battle does call me
To fight as every valiant soldier should.
In the streets then the blood will be
    running,
But 'twill never see me forget thee.'

But Rio Jack wasted no time in listening. If

his plan was to succeed at all he must talk with Villa without delay. As he had expected, he found the general still seated in the main room of the casa. He looked up with a scowl as Rio Jack came in and saluted.

'We showed them dirty slackers how we do things, eh?'

'We sure did,' Rio Jack agreed, forcing into his voice a tone of admiration he did not feel. 'When you figurin' to leave for camp?'

'Pretty soon. Now look here, friend. What you got on your mind?'

'I been doin' some high-powered thinkin',' Rio Jack drawled slowly. 'To tell you the truth, General, I'm kind of worried about Concho Corva an' them papers you sent him after. About the papers, mostly. What's goin' to happen if he gets caught by Nafarrate?'

'*Carramba!* I had forgotten all about that!' Villa's restless eyes flung round the room in searching stabs. 'If Nafarrate gets those papers hell is going to pop!'

'What I figured. Now here's what I was thinkin', General. You give me ten of your soldiers, put 'em in civilian clothes, an' I'll lead them back over our trail an' see if we can't get wind of Corva. We might even get him out of Nafarrate's clutches in case he's been snagged.'

'Now that's an idea, friend. You got a head on your shoulders. You take what men you want and get going pronto. By God, I can't afford to lose them papers, and that's a fact!'

159

'One other thing—I want that spy we caught.'

'What spy is that?'

'The Guzman girl,' Rio Jack said firmly.

Villa's tiger eyes blazed suddenly below his mop of tawny hair. 'What is this you say?'

Rio Jack's steady glance was unreadable as agate. 'I want the Guzman girl to go with me.'

'Why?' the single word fairly purred across the silence.

'Well, it's like this. If I find that Nafarrate's already collared Corva, we can worm into his confidence by havin' that girl with us. We can force her to play our game and introduce us as friends or aids of hers. Then when the chance breaks right, we grab the girl an' Corva an' fan dust for your camp.'

'Oh. But how do you know she won't play you for a sucker? How can you fix it so that, once in Nafarrate's camp, she won't go back on you?'

'Leave that to me, General,' chuckled Rio Jack, getting just the correct amount of brag into his voice. 'I got a way with women. Don't worry, I won't take no dangerous chances with no fool filly. Hell, I ain't aimin' to have Nafarrate stand me up against a 'dobe wall! You lend me the girl, General, an' I'll handle her all right.'

Villa rose from his chair and began to pace the room. Rio Jack hoped he was weighing the plan's chances of success, rather than the

160

question of whether or not he was to be trusted.

A soldier appeared in the doorway. Villa whirled. 'Get ten men out of their uniforms and into civilian clothes—vaquero outfits. Provide them with the best *caballos* in this place. When all is ready come back and tell me. And—hurry!'

Rio Jack drew a long breath. It began to look as though his ruse would work.

'Listen close, friend,' said Villa, and proceeded to describe the encampment he was heading for and a number of ways by which Rio Jack could reach it. When he had finished Rio Jack nodded and said:

'I have had a woman fix her feet up a bit. You know she was without boots when she was captured. Would it be possible for us to get her some boots, a hat, an' a new shirt?'

'I guess it could be arranged,' said Villa, scratching his forehead. 'But why go to such trouble for a damned spy?'

'We don't want her to look like a prisoner in case we have to go into Nafarrate's camp, do we? If he sees her in her present condition and the eleven men with her fully equipped he'll think something's screwy right away.'

'All right, friend. You get her whatever she needs,' said Villa, and turned back to his desk, picking up some papers he was scanning when Rio Jack had entered, though the latter had heard some place that the general could not read. If that was so, he certainly managed to

161

put up a good bluff.

Rio Jack went outside and detailed a soldier to hunt up the things he wanted for Nita. While the soldier was doing so, he went to her room, told the sentry he could leave, and stepped inside.

Nita eyed him curiously.

'I've got it fixed,' he told her and his heart thumped faster at the sudden light that flooded her eyes. 'I've fixed it so I'm detailed to hunt up Concho Corva. The General sent him to Satan's Toe last night to look for those papers they thought you had and which I told Villa I had hidden in Ablon's shack. Must be danged important document, if you ask me. I told him that Corva might get caught by Nafarrate, and that I wanted you along in case he had been, so that we could worm our way into the General's confidence until such time as I saw a chance to snake Corva free.'

'And he fell for it?' she asked incredulously.

'Yeah. Like I hinted, them papers are right important—ain't they?'

Her golden eyes searched his face. 'You are such a good liar I don't know why I trust you,' she spoke impulsively. 'And you have a bad name along the border. I—I guess I do trust you though. There is something about you—'

'About those papers,' Rio Jack interrupted, for the time was short.

'Yes, they are important to Villa. They contain the names of civilians who have agreed

162

to furnish him with supplies and money. They are people who are scattered about through the states of Chihuahua and Coahuila.'

'Have you got them on you?'

She hesitated. Her single word was breathless: 'Yes.'

'I hate to think of you carryin' them around. If Villa knew you had them on you he'd have us both shot pronto.'

'If we see Nafarrate, I'll pass them on,' she promised.

'Why not just destroy them?'

'You do not understand. As long as Villa has support the revolution will go on and on. The only way to stop it is to stop Villa himself.'

'Isn't that the job of Carranza's soldiers?'

'Yes. But Villa is too smart for them. It must be done some other way. There is talk,' she confided, 'of asking intercession of the United States.'

He eyed her curiously. 'Surely Mexico would never appeal to outside aid?'

'It is the only way. No one has ever been able to control Villa long. That is why the President broke with him after making him Commander-in-Chief of our armies. He is pure brute—he is like a pet gorilla. One never knows what he will do next.'

A sudden commotion in the street drew their eyes to the window. A horseman was just dismounting before the casa. Soldiers were running toward him. As Rio Jack made out the mahogany-hued face with its dark, smouldering eyes, its hawk's beak and trap-like lips, his jaw clenched hard.

The man outside was Nevada Ablon!

CHAPTER FOURTEEN

OUT OF THE FRYING PAN—

'Ablon!' whispered the girl.

'Yeah—Nevada Ablon,' Rio Jack grinned crookedly. 'The bad penny that always turns up.'

'Do you know him?'

'Well, I know him good enough. He's a crooked snake if there ever was one. There ain't nothin' he wouldn't do, I reckon, if the dinero weighed sufficient.'

The Nevadan's presence at this time, he reflected, must have given the Devil a hearty laugh. Nothing could be more dangerous to him or to his plans and his standing with Villa than Ablon's presence.

'You knew I got the papers from him, didn't you?'

'I guessed as much,' he admitted. 'I told Villa that you forced Ablon to surrender the papers at the point of a gun.'

Despite the gravity of the situation, a tiny tinkle of laughter left her parted lips. 'That's too funny. He sold out Villa—gave them to me voluntarily in exchange for money.'

'He's sure got a nerve turnin' up here, then. I'll tell you, Nita. His bein' here is goin' to be uncommon hard on us. You can't very well expose him without tippin' our hand. An' he can sure put us in the soup plenty.'

'How?' she asked quickly. 'What can he say? In the first place he probably doesn't know you're here. And even if he learns I'm here, I doubt if he can make matters any worse than they already are.'

'You don't know that polecat very well,' Rio Jack said gruffly. 'He'll make things plenty hot if he learns I'm here. Don't ever doubt it. I've been tryin' to catch up with him to square an old account for the last four years.'

She regarded him thoughtfully. 'Couldn't we get away without him seeing us?'

'Well, we can try, I reckon. Here comes a fellow with some boots for you. I told him to get a hat and a new shirt for you, too. I'll leave while you get fixed up. Ablon will probably go straight to Villa to explain how come he lost those papers. I'll go out an' join my men—'

'What men?' she cut in.

'Oh. I forgot to tell you, I guess, but Villa has provided me with an escort of ten soldiers.'

The golden eyes grew cloudy. 'How will we make our escape with Villa's soldiers watching us?'

'Don't you worry about that,' he grinned. 'I

165

got it all figured out. Soon as you get ready, stay here by the window so you can see me. I'll be outside with my men. Soon as you see me raise my hand to my hat you come runnin' out an' we'll fan dust. If we're lucky mebbe we'll get away before Ablon knows we're here. Or at any rate before he can slip a spoke in our wheel.'

He went to the door, took the things from the soldier and dismissed him. 'Here's the shirt, hat, an' boots,' he said, and tossed them on the bed. 'Remember—when you see me raise my hand, you come a-runnin'.'

When he went out, closing the door behind him, she was already getting out of the grey woollen shirt she had worn across the river. Knowing that she would be ready in a few moments, Rio Jack headed at once for the place where the ten soldiers he had asked for were to assemble.

He found six of them already waiting, sitting loosely in their saddles smoking brown paper cigarettes. They grinned as they saw him coming. Plainly they regarded the prospective scouting trip as something of a lark. To a man they were clad in the range togs of Mexican cowboys. Lean and brown and sinewy, they certainly looked the part, he thought.

'What's happened to the other four?' he asked as he joined them and swung up into the saddle of the long-legged sorrel he and the girl had ridden last night.

166

'They're dickering with a fellow about some horses,' one of the men laughed.

'What's the matter with the ones they were riden?'

'The Chief gave orders that we were to have the fastest mounts in the place,' the man said 'and we sure aimed to have them.'

That was right. Rio Jack recalled the orders Villa had given the soldier. He was mighty glad right now that those orders had been given for they offered him a break.

He glanced around, saw that Ablon's horse was standing nearby. It was a good looking animal, but was not as good as those the vaquero-garbed men forked. He motioned to the nearest man.

'Go see how much longer they're goin' to be arguin',' he directed. 'Hustle them up. I'm in a hurry.'

The man saluted and was about to ride off when Rio Jack snapped:

'Leave the horse here and give your legs a treat, hombre. I want these mounts fresh.' It was a lame excuse as he knew, but the man was in no position to question his orders. With a scowl the fellow dismounted and went bow-legging down the road.

Rio Jack waited until he was out of sight, listening absently to the jokes of the man's companions. But as soon as the walker had disappeared from view he raised his right hand to his hat.

A moment later Nita came running towards them.

Luck was playing strongly in his favour, but he dared not risk another moment's delay. 'Up into the saddle,' he growled at the girl, and jerked his thumb at the departed rider's horse.

No sooner had she mounted than Rio Jack cast a hurried look about and snapped:

'We can't wait any longer for them other birds. Let's go!'

Seven pairs of spurs flashed in the sunlight; seven quirts descended whistling. The horses lunged forward in a bunch. Up the street Rio Jack led the way at a headlong gallop and out upon the burning sands of the desert where heat waves rose and fell in shimmering undulations.

Arcs of glistening sand leapt out behind the horses' pounding feet. Octopus arms of *ocatillo* tipped with crimson blossoms, clumps of *cholla*, prickly pear, and creosote brush spun blurringly past on either side of the plunging horsemen. And the rhythmic roll of the sorrel's muscles between his legs was a movement not one half so swift as the beat of Rio Jack's hammering heart.

From the town they were obscuring in a haze of yellow dust rose shouts, curses and a scattered burst of gunfire.

'Ride, hombres, ride!' gritted Rio Jack.

The vaquero-garbed riders leaned low across their horses' necks and yelled the cry of the ranchers. The shrill yells and the whistling *romals* slashing hard across their flanks wrung added speed from the thundering mounts. The rippled floor of sand streaked past the plunging hoofs in a glistening sheen.

Since Villa had given strict orders that he was to be obeyed, Rio Jack felt little fear of the five soldiers getting out of hand. He knew they must be puzzled by this headlong race and the sound of increasing gunfire from their rear. But that they regarded the whole affair as sport was evident by the flashing grins he had seen in a hurried glance across his shoulder. He was banking heavily on their military training forcing them to obey all orders to the letter regardless of how queer such orders might seem.

'Ride, you saddle-whackers, ride!'

He did not have to be told that if Nevada Ablon had not already poisoned the mind of Villa against him, he would do so shortly. He knew full well the penalty that he and the girl must pay should they again fall into the tawny general's hands.

Among the long odds ranged against him, Rio Jack saw but one thing in their favour. They had a fair start and were straddling the fastest horseflesh of which the town could boast.

'If any of you jaspers know a short cut to Sarizal, speak up quick!' he yelled to make himself heard.

'There ... wash ahead ... bear right ...

169

gypsum sink … Hotter than hell … quickest way I know,' said the rider just behind him; yet close as he was the rush and slap of the wind ripped words from his speech.

Looking dead ahead Rio Jack saw the wash, a dry and shallow depression coursing the sea of sand. He led to the right, skirting it as the man had directed. Half an hour of steady pounding brought into view a great sink in the desert's surface, possibly ten miles from rim to rim.

'Across that?' he yelled, glancing back.

The man who had vouchsafed directions nodded.

Fifteen minutes later they reached the terraced brink leading down into the glaring white waste of the sink. Down a narrow trail that clung precariously to sandstone cliffs the sweating riders picked their way. Now and again they were forced to dismount and lead the horses across some especially treacherous spot.

The trail, sometimes for breath-taking minutes on end, became a thin ribbon of crumbling shale whose outer side was a sheer-walled drop of more than one hundred feet—a one-way passage that was impossible for more than one horse to cross at a time.

Swiftly Rio Jack became aware that if the pursuit reached the rim before he and his men reached the sink's floor it would be a simple matter, and one affording them great pleasure, to pick his riders off with rifles. This fact must be taken into account immediately as it seemed very likely that the pursuit would reach the rim before his party got off that narrow trail.

At the first spot wide enough to permit the turning of a horse, he directed the two rearmost riders to turn their mounts and climb back to a point just below the rim, there to await the arrival of the men bent upon their capture. Because of the great risk they would be incurring, he offered the men he was sending back a bonus of one hundred *pesos* each should they definitely halt pursuit.

When the bonus was to be paid, and by whom, he failed to mention. But the riders chosen did not notice the omission, or if they did were too accustomed to obeying such orders to venture a protest. Rio Jack thought it likely that they expected him to wait for them on the far side of the sink, something he certainly had no notion of doing.

He, the girl, and the three remaining soldiers moved on down the trail. The girl flashed him an approving look for the adroit manner in which he had managed to get rid of two of his escort. He grinned to himself. He knew of ways by which that escort could be whittled down still more.

From time to time he glanced down into the sink. Above its surface hung a snow-white haze of powdered gypsum. Ballooning into the air hundreds of feet above the haze, swirling dust-devils spun shimmering into the east.

As they descended lower the heat grew blistering. Upon the twisting trail the hot smash of the sun struck down like the blow of a monstrous hammer. There was a burning dryness to the air that stung both eyes and nostrils. Their throats felt parched. Their very skin seemed to wither in the searing heat.

With startling suddenness a rattle of rifle fire broke out above them, creating a flat flutter of sound, thin, dry and diminutive in the immensity of the sink.

Rio Jack neither halted nor looked up. Inexorably he pressed his party on; for every added inch of distance put between them and the pursuit widened the girl's chance of ultimate escape.

At last they reached the sink's stifling floor. At a lope they pushed their horses forward and towards the opposite rim. The heat was scorching, breathless. Waves of it rose in shimmering undulations above the glaring waste of gypsum.

Whether the battle on the rim had terminated or not Rio Jack did not know. But no longer was he able to hear the dim, fluttering reports. Steadily they pushed on while the brassy sun above flayed the baking hollow.

The sticky, white grime of the sink coated both mounts and riders. Faces, brows and necks took on the appearance of alabaster masks. Horses grew grey and ghostlike.

After what seemed an interminable space of time they crossed the basin and started the ascent which was easier and more gradual here than the trail they had been forced to travel coming down.

Nevertheless they stopped frequently to rest their heaving animals, for the long trek across the gypsum sink had brought out sweat in a lather that resembled razor-soap about the edges of every saddle blanket.

Yet though the way was easier by far than the descent of the farther rim, it took them longer. It seemed to Rio Jack that they covered miles and miles of twisting twining trails through buckbrush and cedars, star-pines and junipers whose grotesque splintery branches were warped and gnarled. Time and again the trail seemed lost among a maze of mountain-mahogany, but always one of his three remaining troopers succeeded in relocating it.

The stifling afternoon, filled with the resinous scent of evergreen, dragged on interminably. And always the thud of the climbing horses' hoofs made a clattering background for his thoughts.

But at last they reached the rim.

For the first time in hours the girl spoke. Catching him by the arm and stopping both their animals, she pointed into the sunlit distance.

'Look!' she cried. 'Look!'

And following the direction of her pointing

173

arm Rio Jack saw a far-off huddle of box-like adobes, their weathered walls washed golden by the sun.

His grey eyes, reddened by alkali dust, searched her eager face. She shook his arm impatiently.

'It's Sarizal! Your men were right—we've cut the time in half!'

'We ain't there, yet,' he admonished grimly.

'But we'll be there in a coupla hours. Don't look so glum! Aren't you glad we made it?'

'Of course. Shh! Here come the men. Whatever happens they must not get the notion we've got anythin' up our sleeves. I'm aimin' to get rid of two more of 'em right pronto.'

He beckoned the approaching *caballeros*.

'You two,' he said, pointing to the two whom he judged were the best shots of the remaining quartet, 'fork your broncs on into Sarizal from the east while we're enterin' from the southwest. I don't want it to look like you belong to our crowd. Don't stop in Sarizal but cross the bridge and perambulate around over in Gunsmoke. Keep your ears skinned. See if you can learn anythin' about Concho Corva. Also, I'd like to know if Sheriff Silvas is around town.'

The men saluted and turned their horses in a wide arc that would swing them into town from the east.

'You,' Rio Jack addressed the remnant of

his escort, 'go on ahead of us and pick up anything you can about Corva in Sarizal. Find out if he has returned from across the river. If he has, learn which direction he took when he rode out of Sarizal. Meet us around nine o'clock to-night at the Hacienda of the Limping Crow.'

When they were alone Rio Jack faced the girl. 'Our escort is no more,' he grinned. 'We've shucked them easy as rollin' off a log. Now we'll see what we can find out about that Nafarrate assassin. Sure you'll be all right if we meet up with him?'

'But of course. We serve the same interests. Why should he have reason to harm me?'

'Quien sabe?' he answered with a shrug. 'I have no idea. But in times like this it is safest to depend upon no one unless you are intimately acquainted with the gent. Suppose Nafarrate was secretly working with Villa? Your life wouldn't be worth two wags of a horse's tail once you turned over them papers. An' speakin' of them precious documents, why not let me tote 'em for awhile?'

The girl's golden eyes regarded him searchingly as he cuffed the grey dust from his clothes.

Long and earnestly she studied his bronzed features, her face, framed with its lustrous blue-black hair, tilted a bit to one side, her lower lip caught between her teeth, her lovely eyes locked in his.

At last, as though satisfied with what her scrutiny had shown her, she nodded slowly.

'Rio Jack, I am going to trust you fully.' Her voice was low, husky with suppressed emotion. 'If I am mistaken in you then God help us all. I can't give you those papers except as a last resort, but I will tell you that they are intended for the President of the United States.'

'What!' Rio Jack's strong face was a study in startled amazement. 'You tryin' to run on me?'

'Run?' Her lovely eyes grew puzzled.

'I mean is this a joke—?'

'Certainly not. This is too serious a business. I am telling you the truth as the *Señor Dios* is my witness. Pancho Villa is the greatest menace my country has ever faced. The man is a brute—an impulsive, ungovernable beast who kills at will. He must be removed at any cost!

'The Convention determined to relieve him of his command, but had no troops to enforce its will save Villa's own. He laughed at them when they made him Commander-in-Chief. He has sacked, looted, and destroyed. To him there is nothing sacred in this world. He is like some terrible jaguar—no one can guess where next or when he is going to strike!

'If you wish to help my country, or if you have the desire to do something for me, you will help me to place the papers I carry in the hands of your Uncle Sam.'

CHAPTER FIFTEEN

INTO THE FIRE

That Pancho Villa was a primitive force gone beyond the bounds of control, Rio Jack could well appreciate from his contact with the man. But that Mexico would request the aid of the United States in running the man down seemed to him incredible. Yet the impassioned voice and earnest countenance of the girl convinced him of its truth.

Carranza was a menace, too, but evidently the Mexican patriots felt that they could exert more control over him than over the man they had so far supported. It was, he silently agreed, impossible to think of Villa as the bell-mare of any high-minded, reconstructive movement. He could see that even as a military force his limitations were such that dealing with him was like playing ball with a cup of nitroglycerine. Plainly the patriots' patience had become exhausted and they were now determined to crush him at any cost.

'Well,' he said at last, 'I'll certainly help you all I can, Nita. I ain't got a notion who you ought to see, but I reckon maybe the Commandant at Fort Bliss could prob'bly help you. Anyway, he'll know who you oughta see. We'll go to him.'

He paused to shove back his broad-brimmed *charro* hat and run a hand through his yellow curls. 'Point is, how to get to El Paso. Far as I can see, we'll just have to stick to the brush. We can't risk headin' that way openly. Villa has spies all around the border country. We got to be doggone careful, girl. It's gonna be sure death 'f we get caught.'

'You're going to help me,' a glad light showed for a moment in her golden eyes. Something else, too, which he found it hard to define, but which nevertheless set his pulses racing like a heady wine.

'Well, I sure aim to try a heap,' he told her frankly.

She extended her hand, let it lay for a glorious moment in his own rope-scarred fist. Only by a mighty effort of his will did he keep from blurting out his love.

But she must have read it in his glance. She blushed, said swiftly:

'I think we'd better go.'

For seconds his eyes beat hard against her, but she would not look.

'All right,' he said flatly, forcing all emotion from his tone. 'Be better if we could steer clear of Sarizal an' Gunsmoke, but I reckon it just ain't in the cards. We got to cross that toll bridge. With half a break we'll make it, too. But if anything happens you keep goin'.'

She faced him swiftly in cold alarm. 'And leave you? What will *you* do?'

His wide lips parted letting his teeth flash in a satanic grin. 'I'll burn powder.'

'While I ride free? Listen—I brought you into this. I won't run out on you. Either we fight this thing together else we part right now. It's your move.'

He gazed into the determined oval of her sun-tanned face. He drew a deep breath. 'All right. Shake, pard,' he said with reservations he deemed it best not to mention.

Once again she placed her warm smooth hand in his big calloused one. They turned their horses then and headed towards the river whose location in the distance was marked by silver thread.

They rode at a fast lope, yet even so the sun was dropping behind the blue-black Yankee Peaks ere they reached its brush-lined bank. With never a moment's pause they followed the Rio Grande south and jogged into Sarizal just as Night dropped its sable blanket across the border range.

The sinister gleam of occasional street lamps but served to thicken the squalid murk that lay across the adobe town.

Rio Jack and Nita now rode forward at a slow walk lest the hurried hoofbeats of their mounts arouse suspicion. Slowly they drew nearer the bridge that led to Yankeeland.

As ever when danger threatened a pulse beat fast in the throat of Rio Jack. Yet, judging from his tranquil exterior, none would ever

179

have guessed that an inner excitement gripped him as they neared the international bridge.

With the coming of darkness a chill wind had whipped up off the plains. Now, as they neared he last adobe on the riverward side of town, from around it the gusty wind drove a flurry of muttered conversations.

'Bound to ... this way. Pedro said ... up the soldiers in pairs. It's a cinch they're ... jump the country.'

The voice was Concho Corva's!

The girl checked her horse. Rio Jack reined in his sorrel close beside her. Leaning outward from the saddle he placed his lips beside her ear.

'They're waitin' for us,' he whispered. 'Somehow Corva an' some of our escort got together. Reckon Nafarrate didn't stick around long or Corva wouldn't be here. Don't know how many he's got with him, but our only chance will be a rush. When I give you the signal, dig in your spurs. An' don't stop for the Mex inspection or we'll burn our hash sure as God makes little apples!'

In the darkness he saw the vague oval of her face nod twice. He drew his long-barrelled guns from the half-breed holsters.

'*Now!*' he gritted, and sank his spurs.

Both horses lunged forward toward the bridge like bolts from a single cross-bow. As they passed the far corner of the adobe building a gun exploded viciously, drove a leaping crimson slash across the murk. Lead whined above their heads. Neither stopped nor faltered.

Behind the corner as they swept past, Rio Jack beheld the vague outlines of crouched, steeple-hatted figures. His guns threw lead in bursting arcs as the hammers dropped beneath his thumbs.

Cries, oaths, shouts and the harsh clump of running feet intermingled with the raucous crash of gunfire. One blurred figure jackknifed and went down, a second reeled crazily in the gloom, clutching at his chest. Then the fugitives were clear and thundering down upon the plank bridge.

The pounding hoofs of the hard-spurred broncs lashed up the roaring echoes as they drummed out on to the sun-warped boards; echoes that swallowed the distant pop of guns whose lead fell short.

Now they were sweeping into the lighted area by the guardhouse where stood the inspection officials of the Mexican Government. Two khaki-clad officers with ready rifles sprang from the shack to the centre of the passage.

Rio Jack and the girl slowed momentarily as though to a stop. They could see the grim expressions of the rifle-holders slacken. Rio Jack's triggerless pistols rose in a burst of lurid flame as again their spurs bit hard.

The right-hand officer crashed down upon

his back. His companion reeled, whirled half around by the impact of gringo lead. He regained his balance and brought his rifle up. Fire spurted from its muzzle. A ball smashed against the sorrel's saddle horn, splattered in bits of flying lead.

Rio Jack's long-barrelled weapons crashed again and the man went down with a sobbing curse.

Across the narrow bridge they pounded, sending out a hoof-drummed clatter that drowned the pandemonium behind. The girl's set face held grim resolve that yet was mild beside the tight-lipped scowl of Rio Jack as, with shaking fingers, he jammed fresh cartridges into his smoking guns.

Yet even as he filled their heated chambers he saw three soldiers dart to the American end of the bridge. They knelt in unison and brought rifles to their shoulders, sighting down their barrels.

'We'll never make it!' cried the girl. 'It is madness to go on!'

He knew her words were true, but refused stubbornly to admit it.

'Do you hear me?' she panted. 'It is death to go on!'

'Yeah—an' death to go back. We got to make it, girl. It's our only chance. Lean low across your bronc's neck an' kick your feet from the stirrups. If they drop the horse he'll fling you clear. Straight at 'em now!'

Lead whined shrill as tiny bursts of smoke ballooned above the motionless hats of the kneeling soldiers.

'That's a warnin',' gritted Rio Jack, and raked his mount with dripping spurs.

They had taken the Mexicans by surprise. He gave the fact due credit for their success in getting past. But yonder kneeling figures were both ready and waiting, he could almost see the tensity with which curled fingers caressed the cold steel of rifle triggers. Another score of paces would mean sheer suicide!

He found it bleak, bitter bleak, to realize that there was no other way. If they were to elude both the obstacle and pursuit, they must needs ride those waiting figures down.

A physical sickness clutched him. A mental nausea caused his brain to reel before the knowledge of that awful peril into which he, by his own example, was forcing this girl to go. Not for himself was Rio Jack afraid, but for her who rode at his side with resolute chin and blanching cheeks.

'Listen, God,' he breathed in desperation, 'I've never asked for much, but—' the rest went unsaid as a vision of Nita's willowy body stretched outsprawled on the moon-drenched planks, bullet-torn and ghastly, flashed vividly before his mind.

Vital as he knew it to be to their plans to cross to the American shore without pause or hindrance, he realized abruptly that he could

183

not go through with this mad dash. He could not do it, he told himself. Despite all that was at stake, and he knew the possible fate of a nation to be hanging in the balance, he could not bring himself to lead the girl he loved to death. Fate was asking too much of flesh and blood!

His hands sheathed the triggerless pistols they were holding. His left shot out and closed about the bridle of Nita's horse while his right, palm forward, rose above his head in token of surrender. When he had brought the horses to a definite stop he found themselves within thirty feet of the kneeling waiting soldiers, whose light-limned features loomed harsh and bleak.

'Advance your horses at a walk,' growled a sergeant from the side. 'One false move, hombres, an' we'll drop you like a flash!'

Rio Jack urged his sorrel forward at a funereal pace, while in his ears rang the frantic shouts of Corva, whose boots he could hear pelting after them across the bridge.

He did not turn his head, nor did his level grey eyes refuse to meet the sergeant's angry scowl. He even grinned a little, while his ragged yellow brows arched mockingly above his saturnine glance.

'Bad time to be shovin' on the reins, Sarg,' he advised the scowling officer. 'Every split fraction of a second you delay us is goin' to be that much tougher for you later on. You're stoppin' mighty important folk, if you only

184

knew it.'

'Obregon an' Carraanza, I guess you'll tell me,' the sergeant jeered.

'Shucks—no small fry like that. We're couriers to the President.'

'Yeah? What president? Ulalio?'

'Woodrow Wilson.'

'Horsefeathers! You can't saw that off on me—'

'Show him your papers, pardner.'

One of Nita's small hands slipped inside her skirt, came out with a long white envelope heavily sealed in red wax with the Eagle and the Serpent. Hesitantly she passed it to the sergeant, who took it closer to the lights.

The booted feet of Corva and his henchmen were drawing close. The bumping heart of Rio Jack told him that their time was nearly up. Once Corva joined the confab their end would loom in sight...

'Don't let them *jibaros* pass!' Corva's yell came wailing down the wind.

CHAPTER SIXTEEN

'IT'S THAT HELL-A-MILER GOLDEN!'

'That shoutin' gent is Concho Corva, the Mex bandit,' said Rio Jack with sudden grimness. 'You'll hold us, Sergeant, at your peril!'

The sergeant chuckled. 'Mebbeso. But you can bet I'll hold you just the same. I'm going to know all about that shootin' an' everything else before I pass you two into the States. For all I know, this document,' he tapped the sealed envelope 'is a fake.'

'Fake or not, you give it back to the lady pronto.'

'Huh! *Lady!*' the sergeant stared then touched his hat. 'Well, I'll be dadgummed! What you two pullin' anyhow? This an elopement or somethin'?'

Rio Jack had slowly been urging his sorrel forward, inch by cautious inch. Nita had been following suit. They were close beside the sergeant again as he asked his questions.

'It's somethin', all right,' grunted Rio Jack ominously. 'An' if you don't get us off this bridge before them fellows get here, your name's gonna be mud!'

'You tryin' to threaten me?'

Rio Jack shot a look over his shoulder. The running Corva was but twenty feet away, and behind him came several other steeple-hatted figures! Plainly it was now or never, he thought desperately.

Leaning forward in the saddle, his right fist lashed out. It caught the sergeant in the throat as his left hand snatched the sealed packet from the officer's lax fingers. As the sergeant reeled sideways, spurs dug deep and the fugitives' horses lunged forward past the startled soldiers who had been standing at attention.

'Duck low an' don't spare that nag!'

Rio Jack had had no real hope of escape when he struck the sergeant. But now he began to wonder as they pounded off the bridge whether after all they might not yet win free.

A pistol cut through the oaths and shouted orders churning up behind. The ball tore through his hat as he hunched lower in the saddle and gave the sorrel its head; Corva had taken that shot, he thought, but he kept his eyes fixed on the stretch of sand that lay between the bridge and the town of Gunsmoke towards which their mounts were heading.

Rifles cracked with vicious spite, hurling lead through the moonlit night about them.

'Are you hit?' came huskily from Nita.

'No. You?'

'Not yet.'

'Good girl. Swing for that patch of shadow up ahead. We'll not go through the town unless we have to.'

A clump of junipers thirty yards ahead offered temporary shelter from the whining lead that cut the night about them. They swung towards the welcome shadows with the shouts of the angry sergeant ringing in their ears and the smooth-rolling muscles of their gallant mounts between their legs.

Twenty feet from the junipers the girl's horse staggered. Her booted feet kicked free of the stirrups as it went crashing down, flinging her from the saddle. Face down in the sand she fell and did not move.

Cold fear clutched the pounding heart of Rio Jack as he jerked the sorrel to a slithering halt. He was out of the saddle and beside her in a moment. Swiftly he stooped and lifted her in his arms. He gasped endearing names to her as he hugged her against his chest while flying lead cut the sand about him. He cursed softly when her eyes refused to open and he saw how white and drawn was the oval of her face.

He was still cursing as he went lurching towards his horse. He lost all track of time as he fought to gain the saddle with his burden. But somehow he made it and eventually found himself beyond the juniper's shadow. His heart was thudding wildly as he drew rein to scan his surroundings and take stock of the situation.

'Sort of looks like I'm losin' my technique,' he muttered grimly. If the girl would only waken—

He glanced anxiously at the pale sweet face so close to his own, and as he looked her eyes came fluttering open. Their liquid golden depths became serene and tranquil with a trusting calm as they picked out his rugged moonlit features.

'Are you bad hurt, Nita, honey?' his voice was husky with emotion.

A faint smile quirked the corners of her scarlet lips. 'Of course I'm not—just shook up a little from my fall,' she snugged against his

188

shoulder and, despite their unenviable plight, he felt a surge of ecstacy such as he had never known. She *did* trust him, he thought with throbbing pulses.

'Are we safe now?'

'Not yet,' he muttered, and his lean jaw grew hard and rigid as he recalled the danger that surrounded them. There was no man in this town he could call friend; every man's hand seemed to be against him, trying to pull him down. At any moment pursuit from off the bridge might come crashing through the junipers. He could hear Corva's snarling voice, could sense its growing nearness.

Yet if he attempted to skirt the town he reflected that the chances were around a thousand to one of their ever getting clear. Before they could put a rise between themselves and the pursuit they were bound to be spotted in the moonlight's argent arc. Better by far, he thought, to risk the chance of recognition in the town. So thinking, he kneed the sorrel towards the yellow pools of light that seeped from Gunsmoke's open doors and windows.

'Where are we going?' Nita breathed against his cheek.

'It's early yet an' there'll be a heap of jaspers on the street,' he answered softly. 'Our best chance, as I see it, is to leave this bronc *muy pronto* an' try to lose ourselves in the crowd.'

He turned the sorrel into an opening

between two adobe buildings. 'Reckon you can walk?'

'Of course. I'm not one of those sugar-and-spice girls. Let me down and I'll prove it.'

She slid from the horse as he released her and he swung from the saddle beside her. Swiftly he debated the pros and cons of whether or not it was better to say '*Adios*' to the sorrel gelding. If they left it here it might be found. Yet he hesitated to drive the animal off for fear they might yet have further need of its services.

On the other hand, if they drove the sorrel out into the desert the pursuit might be confused as to where they had left its back.

He caught Nita's inquiring eyes upon him and made his decision. This was no place for them to linger. Slapping the horse smartly across the rump, he sent it galloping off across the moonlit sand.

He tucked his arm in hers then and they went strolling nonchalantly into Gunsmoke's single street and joined the boisterous crowd that thronged its board walks to overflowing.

No one was looking towards the river, he noted, and judged from the apparent indifference displayed that if the shots at the bridge had been noted at all, they had been thought to mark some minor shooting affray that would not be worth the trouble of looking into.

But that, he realized, meant nothing in their favour. The soldiers would start combing the town before very long. Even if they did not, Corva's hellions certainly would!

'What happens now?'

He glanced at her obliquely. Her cheeks were no longer pale and her eyes seemed to have regained their accustomed sparkle. Could it be possible, he wondered, that she did not see the awful peril their escape from the bridge had placed them in?

Two plans lay open to Rio Jack. They were sauntering along in the crowd, gradually drawing nearer to the Singing Stopper. They could continue to meander along in this desultory fashion until they should come upon two fast pieces of horseflesh suitable to long and enduring flight. Or they could go at once to the Sheriff's Office and, explaining that they were messengers to the high authorities of the United States, demand Silvas's protection.

Rio Jack's wide lips framed a sardonic grin. The protection the swarthy pock-marked sheriff of Gunsmoke would offer them did not loom at all pleasant or desirable in his mind. The first plan, he decided, was the best. It was none too good, but it was their only chance so far as he could see.

'We'll drift along with the crowd for a while,' he answered the girl's question.

'Won't that be dangerous? What if you are recognized as the man Silvas was bent on hanging?'

'Time enough to worry about that after I'm

recognized. If we break loose of this crowd we'll be spotted pronto by Corva's men. They must have guessed by now that we're in town. Ain't a very good bet, Nita, but I can't figure nothin' better. The cards are dealt an' it's up to us to do the best we can.'

She nodded and a sudden smile lit up her face. 'Odds don't mean much to you, do they?'

'Shucks,' he said, but her compliment warmed him none the less. 'Fellow can't often get what he wants. He's got to take what he gets an' like it. Whether the game's bein' dealt from a cold deck or not, it's up to us players to do the best we can with the hand we're given.'

'That's a good philosophy,' she approved. 'I like it.'

A faint blush washed his bronzed cheeks at her praise. 'Sho, you take it pretty well yourself,' he answered warmly.

'Not the same thing. I'm getting paid to do what I do. Besides, I'm working in the interests of my country as I see them. You have no object in—I mean, what you are doing is being done without hope of reward. You are risking your life to help me just because I got you out of Silvas's jail. It is not necessary for you to take any further chances on my account. I rescued you from Silvas because you helped me out at Satan's Toe. There can be no hope of my government rewarding you—'

'Shucks, you'd be surprised what I'm hopin' for,' he cut in. Then grinning: 'You ain't married by any chance, are you?'

A faint colour livened her cheeks. She turned her face to the front and refused to meet his twinkling eyes.

'Are you?' he persisted.

She bit her lip. 'No,' she answered finally.

'Nor engaged?'

'No-o-o, but—'

'Then the hand's worth playin' out, the way I look at it,' he said definitely, and his pulses leaped as she met his eyes for a fleeting instant before turning her face ahead again.

She suddenly stopped and he felt her body stiffen. As his gaze swept up he saw the colour leave her face and her eyes grow swiftly narrow. He swung his glance ahead.

A gold-bespangled steeple-crowned sombrero was weaving towards them through the crowd that thronged the narrow walk. No need to ask whose hat it was, for he knew it instantly for Corva's. And that the man had spotted them was proved by the dexterous speed with which his hat bobbed nearer.

There was one thing in their favour. Corva dared not use his gun for fear of hitting someone else and starting a general battle. Grabbing the girl's arm Rio Jack swung her round. 'Catch hold of my belt and hang on tight!' he grunted and, turning, began threading his way through the jostling groups of sauntering cowpokes, gamblers and townsmen back over the way they had just now come.

After several hurrying moments he asked:

'Still following?'

Her panted answer was lost in the noisy crowd. He spoke again:

'Corva still behind?'

'Yes,' he caught her answer this time, 'I think he's gaining. People are beginning to turn around.'

That was all right, in fact it was exactly what he wanted. He thought: 'Let 'em turn.'

In a deliberate effort to pile up trouble for the pursuing Corva, he grew less gentle in shoving men aside, and his elbows brought grunts from the gents who moved too slowly. Usually the grunters were large men, fellows who would be unlikely to stand for such tactics twice in the same stretch of walk. He moved briskly forward with the girl in tow behind.

Suddenly he felt his belt yanked sharply and wheeled. 'What's up?'

She nodded backward. 'Corva's gotten into a fight with a big cowhand.'

'That's sad as hell,' he muttered pleasantly. 'Let's mosey on in case the fireworks start.'

But hardly had they gone ten steps when oaths in two languages and the meaty thud of flesh on flesh announced that the fight was on in earnest. The crowd stampeded towards the scene of action, catching Rio Jack and the girl in their mad scramble and carrying them along.

'Damn greaser dog!' the big cowpoke

growled. 'You need a lesson in manners an' by Gawd yo're gonna git one!'

'Gringo pig! You would not dare touch one of Pancho Villa's staff!'

'The hell you say!' and the big cowboy's fist crashed against the Mexican's chest with a force that flung him backward. 'You ain't across the river now—an' far as that goes, all the damn Spics in Coahuila couldn't give me a chill!'

Concho Corva whipped out an eight-inch blade and charged. Yet before he could reach the big cowpoke, a bystander knocked the knife from his grasp.

A flood of vile invective fell from the Mexican's twisted lips. His hand swept down for his gun.

'Why, you orn'ry louse!' growled the cowboy, and charged head down with flailing arms.

Rio Jack felt almost sorry for Corva then. Before the Mexican could yank his pistol clear of leather, the big puncher was upon him, pummelling his swarthy face with battering fists.

Gasping, cursing, Corva fought as best he could, but it was evident at once that he was no good match for the big American. The puncher's hammering fists seemed everywhere at once. One buried itself in the Mexican's stomach and as he bent double with pain another rock-hard fist came up and smacked

195

against his jaw. Corva went over backwards into the dusty street.

But he was not finished yet. Hardly had he hit the street than his gun was out of leather. A streak of crimson darted from its muzzle. The big cowboy staggered. A look of blank astonishment broke over his craggy feature. Then he was down on one knee and his own gun was spitting leaden death.

'Quick!' Rio Jack said, grabbing the girl and joining a number of the bystanders who, with the bark of pistols ringing danger, were breaking for the open. 'This is no place for us. There's goin' to be the devil to pay in about one-an'-a-half split-seconds!'

They joined the nervous bystanders' sprint for safety, though not because they were afraid of flying lead. And as they ran the buildings on either side flung back the crash of thundering guns to intermingle with the scuffle of booted feet and the shouts and oaths of running men.

The street was in an uproar yet Rio Jack hesitated to leave it for the open country behind its frame and adobe buildings for fear the soldiers might be scouting there. As he told the girl in hurried words:

'This ain't no place for folks like us to be right now. But behind them houses might be a whole heap worse. We'll stick to the street and make for the Sangre de Oro. Ablon's got a hole-up there we'll duck into till the excitement blows away.'

196

Catching her hand he took to the 'outlaws' sidewalk'—the centre of the street. Except for a number of vehicles hurriedly deserted when the shooting started, the road was clear and offered the handiest means of unimpeded progress.

They managed to get within forty feet of their objective without hindrance. But not one step farther in that direction did they take. From around the far corner of the Sangre de Oro came three running hombres pelting for the scene of the shooting. With narrowing eyes Rio Jack took in the flash of metal on their vests.

'Quick!' he gritted. 'Back the way we came. That's Silvas an' his deputies!'

As they turned a door opened nearby and threw a flood of light across their faces. Silvas's bull roar came ringing down the wind:

'My Gawd! It's that hell-a-miler Golden! After 'im boys! Five-hundred bucks to the gent what brings him down!'

CHAPTER SEVENTEEN

GUNFLAME AND MOONLIGHT

'Slide down that alley pronto!' Rio Jack poked a hand towards an opening between two buildings on the Satan's Toe side of the street.

197

The girl veered into it and he followed on her heels, thankful that the angle of the right-hand building effectively lopped off all sight of them from the pursuing lawmen.

'Like ol' times, our running from Silvas and Company,' Rio Jack chuckled grimly. 'Like playin' tag or follow the leader.'

'Only if he tags us,' Nita panted as she ran, 'we'll be out of the game for keeps.'

'An' that sure ain't no lie!'

'Where do we go from here?'

They had reached the far end of the passage between the buildings. The desert opened before them. Rio Jack thrust his head from the alley's mouth and flashed swift glances in either direction. He saw a tiny lean-to built against the rear of the left-hand house.

He jerked a thumb towards it imperatively. 'Get behind there quick!' his incisive words were curt as, with a shove, he sent her towards it. Whirling then he dashed about the corner of the right-hand house and waited, big hands curled about the butts of his holstered six-guns.

Even before he got in position he could hear the pounding boots of Silvas and his two companions, whom he guessed to be Pring and Cimarron Charlie. The next moment they burst from the alley's mouth.

'Hold it, gents!'

As Rio Jack's cool drawling voice fell athwart their path the three sprinting lawmen skidded to a halt as though checked by a hemp

198

lasso. With ludicrous expressions they froze in their tracks, and the forward-thrust of their hands were of no more use at that moment than so many sticks.

Silvas ripped out a vile oath.

'Shh! be careful, Sheriff. There's a lady present,' warned Rio Jack, and could not resist humming:

'There was a gent in Gunsmoke Town,
Was rated wondrous wise—
Yet he leaped into some chaparral
An' scratched out both his eyes!'

Silvas snorted. 'You'll sing soft, fella, before I'm done with you,' he threatened. 'You put it over on me once—'

'How about this time?'

'This time ain't finished yet!'

'It will be soon, though,' Rio Jack told him. He raised his voice:

'Pard, come relieve these statues of their hardware. I can see their hands are gettin' plumb tired holdin' up them smoke-poles.'

Nita, her hat brim drawn low across her eyes, came forward silently to collect the lawmen's weapons. Silvas gave her a scowling look, but because of the shadows apparently did not realize that she was not a man. Cimarron Charlie shifted his feet restlessly.

'Keep tame, gents,' Rio Jack advised softly. 'First hombre that blinks crooked is goin' to get his light snuffed out.'

When the girl had taken the weapons from their hands she backed away. Rio Jack dared not attempt a search for hide-out guns. Time was too precious. Nor did he dare to hold them longer. He was in the unenviable position of the man who had the bull by the tail. He hated to let go, yet on the other hand he dared not hold on longer.

'All right, face back the way you came,' he ordered curtly. 'Fine. Now up it, gents. *Vamonos!*'

Silvas snarled a final threat: 'You'll never git outa this town, wise guy!'

'Maybe I ain't wantin' to,' Rio Jack said coldly. 'Light out, hombres, an' don't come back unless you come a-smokin'.'

The sheriff and his deputies strode down the narrow alley. Before they reached the street, Rio Jack and the girl were cat-footing it for another opening three houses down the street. They slipped into it without detection.

Placing his lips close to the girl's ear, he said:

'Ought to be headin' for the saloon like we was before, but it's too dangerous now. Knowin' we was headin' up the street when they bumped into us, Silvas and Company will be streakin' that way pronto soon as they get some hardware.'

'What will we do?'

'Light a shuck outa here quick as we can locate some ground-eatin' horseflesh,' he replied. 'But we won't mosey into the street just yet. Silvas *might* be lookin' for some such play. Best to play it safe an' wait a spell.'

'We do have the worst kind of luck,' she whispered.

'Sho, it ain't so bad. We're still in the game an' we got one or two chips left even yet. Things could be a whole lot worse, pardner.'

'Yeah—that's right,' wisked an ominous voice from the shadows of a greasewood clump behind them. 'I reckon yuh still got them papers on yuh. Jest dig 'em up an' lay 'em on the ground there in that patch o' moonlight, then sift along outa the alley!'

Rio Jack whirled and flame licked out from his crouching hips. Gun barks lashed up the roaring echoes, the adobe walls slapped them back and forth. Shoving the girl ahead of him, he hurried down the alley towards the street, not daring to linger along enough to learn whether his lead had done its work for fear that the shooting would be drawing Silvas and his men.

'Who was it?' Nita gasped.

'Sounded like that half-cracked hombre they call Mexico,' he answered, busily refilling the empty chambers of his pistol. 'If it was, it means that those jaspers we lost in the sink have caught up with us. An' that means that Nevada Ablon's someplace around this town!'

They reached the alley's mouth and heard the spur-jingling sound of running boots converging. Rio Jack caught her arm. 'This is goin' to be a tight spot in about two shakes. We got to fan dust pronto or they'll nail our pelts on the fence.'

He pointed towards a nearby hitch rack. 'See that roan broomie [*A dark horse with a long loose, or coarse, heavy tail*], beside the claybank mare? You fork him an' I'll take the claybank. We got to fade quick. It's dangerous, but we got no choice. Neck meat or nothin'. Let's *go!*'

They streaked into the open moonlit street and reached the hitch rack. The girl got the broomtail's reins loose and swung to his saddle. But some cautious gent had tied the claybank's reins more firmly than was the usual habit. As he plucked desperately at the knot it seemed to Rio Jack that his fingers were all thumbs. A shout went up three doors away. Men began to converge on the hitch rack at a run.

'Get away from that horse, you damn thief!' one of the runners yelled, and the gun in his hand spat fire.

Lead tore through the *carro* hat, then the reins came loose in his hands. Rio Jack caught the horn in his left hand. Both horses were running hard when his tight-fitting trousers slapped the saddle.

They bent low across the borrowed horses' necks and their spurs jabbed hard as a rattle of gunfire drowned the snarling voices of cursing men. Lead sang past with a vicious swish. Rio

Jack's impressions were incoherent. Moonlight and shadow spun blurringly past as they tore down the dusty road and raced for the open desert.

Even before they cut loose of town they could hear the muffled thunder of pursuing hoofs, intermingled with the paths and shouts and gunfire.

'Head for Satan's Toe an' don't let nothin' stop you!' he shouted, and reaching inside his shirt he produced the all-important papers which he had snatched from the sergeant's hand. 'Here, take these—I might have to stop!' and he shoved the packet into her reaching hand.

'If you stop for anything, I'll stop too.'

'Yeah? Well, you better not look like it! You been playin' a man's part in this thing long enough. You do as I say or I'll paddle you good first chance I get!'

Despite the seriousness of their situation her scarlet lips parted in a swift tinkling of mirth. Then she sobered. 'If you stop you'll never get the chance,' was her shrewd retort. 'We're in this thing together, Rio Jack, and if you insist on helping me any further we'll share our luck together. What's good enough for one to do is just as good for the other. I don't want you pulling any martyr stunts.'

'Good gosh!' he muttered. 'Nothin' was farther from my mind,' he denied without strict truth. Nevertheless, his blood pounded to her words and that which they implied. Evidently she *did* care at least a little for him, he thought, and his spirits took an upward surge. Gosh! Made a fellow feel like tackling a mountain lion with one hand tied behind his back!

The rush and slap of the wind beat strong against their faces as they struck off across the desert. The moonlit sand gleamed like a silver sea and in the distance lay the silent peaks of dim-seen purple mountains. Now that they had left the turbulent town behind it seemed as though another world encompassed them a world of still and slumbrous beauty.

They rode for an hour with only the wind and the soft beat of their ponies' hoofs for company. The pursuit was still dogging their trail as Rio Jack observed when, from time to time, he flashed a backward look across his shoulder. But if they lost no ground at least they were not gaining. And he felt it imperative to shake the shadowy group of horsemen as soon as possible. It would not be long now till he and Nita were forced to swing west. They had gone north almost as far as he dared.

Silvas's posse had long since ceased to fire. They were evidently intending to conserve their ammunition until such time as a closer range should serve to make it effective. That the pursuit felt they would soon get closer was not, to Rio Jack's way of thinking, a pleasant thought. But he saw no sense in sharing it with the girl.

With cold grey glance he raked the endless sand ahead. Suddenly his face went bleak. The slightest flexure of his fingers upon the reins stopped the claybank instantly. Nita drew rein beside him.

'What is it?' her voice was anxious. 'Why have we stopped?'

To their north the mountains still loomed distant. Westward the Rio Diablo cut a dark gash in the rolling waste, and beyond great cobalt shadows leaned down from the saw-toothed peaks of the range they had to cross.

'How'd you manage to keep them papers dry when we crossed the river the other night?' he countered.

'I keep them in an oilskin packet, pinned to—but does it matter?'

'Yeah. We got to cross the Rio Diablo up ahead to the left there. We got to cross it pronto, too. Look,' his outflung arm pointed north in the direction he had been gazing when they halted. 'See that ridge three-four miles off? Well, watch it close now an' tell me what you see.'

Far away beyond the ridge floated a thin moving line of dust resembling a smudge of smoke because of the distance. As Nita and Rio Jack sat silently watching a file of black dots swiftly crossed the ridge and disappeared.

'Horsemen!'

'Yeah,' Rio Jack's single word held a brittle dryness.

'You think it's someone trying to head us off?'

'You guessed it. The posse must have split.'

'But how could they get around us that way?'

'There's a short cut to Satan's Toe from Gunsmoke. In the excitement it slipped my mind.'

'What'll we do?'

'We can't go that way any further. Listen!'

From the south came the dim flutter of many hoofs. They turned in their saddles, gazing over their back trail. A shadowy group of riders came tearing towards them, their gear metal shooting off bright streaks through the churning murk of dust.

'Can't go back, either.'

The girl's face paled in the moonlight but her golden eyes were steady as she returned Rio Jack's sardonic glance. 'I guess we can't. So—?'

'Exactly. It's neck meat or nothin'. We got to cross the Rio Diablo pronto. If we angle southwest to strike the road they'll nail us. We got to hit straight west. Got to put the river an' them saw-toothed mountains behind us. We better be startin'.'

They turned their horses west and their pounding hoofs ripped up the yellow dust.

For another hour they rode without pause, swerving to neither right nor left but heading straight for the river's gash. As they dropped

206

down its nearer bank they could see that the two factions of the posse had gained, due to their change in direction. The townward faction was now but a scant half mile behind.

They swiftly found a shallow crossing and splashed to the opposite bank. As they clambered up the sloping shale they could hear the exultant shouts of the gaining posse.

'Them jaspers better save their wind,' Rio Jack grunted. 'They ain't got us—yet.'

Time passed in dragging seconds to the rhythmic thud of their ponies' hoofs. They were holding their own again but that was all. Across a silvered plain they moved with wraithlike speed, the animals' falling hoofs still lifting with power and ease, their gallant hearts beating steadily against their riders' knees.

'But they can't last forever,' Rio Jack spoke the thought aloud. 'We can last until they drop. After that—' he shrugged his broad shoulders and dragged the carbine from its scabbard.

'Don't stop yet!'

'Not goin' to. Not yet but soon.'

They were climbing steadily now, mounting the foothills towards the saw-toothed peaks. A half hour passed with only the click of shod hoofs on rock to betray their whereabouts among the clustering shadows. The moon was dropping behind the peaks and the wind had died away. The air was heavy with the resinous scent of pine and juniper.

A night for romance, he thought, and they

were spending it like hunted wolves!

Gradually the trees thinned out. They were getting higher. Twisting in his saddle Rio Jack sent a backward glance along their trail. But the pursuit was enveloped in the shadows and could not be seen. Only the noise of their progress could be dimly heard in the distant crashing of the brush.

The way was more open now with occasional patches of moonlight slithering down between the branches of the scrubby timber.

'Hit south a spell,' he grunted, and swung his horse hoping the posse would keep on due west.

The going grew easier for their new trail was almost level as they circled the towering crags whose rugged peaks were bathed in the hazy glow of the fading moon.

They found a pass and clattered through it, their ponies' feet lashing up the steel-wrung echoes. An owl drifted past on silent wings. They dropped down a narrow canyon, came to a tiny stream and paused to let the horses drink. Sparingly.

They went on again at an easy jog, covering miles of twistings and turnings through buckbrush and cedars. They quartered a gigantic hogback and crossed seemingly uncrossable ravines. A rolling plain lay three hundred yards below them when the dawn was but an hour away.

They paused at the top of a gentle slope shelving down. The horses stood with drooping necks and spraddled legs. They were not done, but Rio Jack realized that they could not go much farther. Fresh horseflesh was in demand.

'Reckon we lost the posse.'

'Not knowing how we ever got through the mountains ourselves,' said Nita wearily, 'I don't see how Silvas's men could possibly have managed to follow us. We must have lost them hours ago. Can't we stop awhile? I'm so sleepy I'm almost falling off.'

'Good kid,' Rio Jack's voice was filled with admiration. 'You stood it like a soldier. Ain't many men could have done as well. Speakin' personal, I feel like a piece of saddle leather.'

'So do I—the curled up kind that's been in the sun a long time. Speaking of the sun, I'll be glad to see it again. Won't you?'

'That depends,' Rio Jack drawled slowly. 'If we've lost the posse I'd just as soon have some sun on the subject. But if they've stuck to our trail or—' he broke off suddenly, tensing in the saddle, big shoulders hunched a little forward, listening.

'What is it—?' she began, when with a curt gesture he motioned her to silence. Minutes dragged past in a deathly hush. Twenty feet away, in a patch of deep shadow, a stick snapped sharply. The brown, scarred hands of Rio Jack curled around the worn pistol butts

209

protruding from his half-breed holsters. His cold unwavering eyes studied the gloom.

A bell of warning clanged in his mind, yet even as he listened to it he knew what he must do. Swiftly he slid from the saddle and cat-footed toward the murky thicket. Almost to it, his alert ears caught a sharp metallic click. He did not have to ask what that sound signified—he knew. Someone had cocked a gun!

'Come outa that, hombre.' Low but vibrant his deep voice cut the silence like a lash. 'An' come *quick*!'

From the midst of the thicket a streak of crimson slashed the murk. With a side leap that was none too soon Rio Jack felt the wind of the unknown's bullet. Then his guns were crashing leaden death, spraying the thicket from side to side. A sobbing cry mingled with the fading echoes as he sprang forward, surging through the brush.

CHAPTER EIGHTEEN

'VILLA'S CAMPED OUTSIDE!'

Fate sometimes hinges on queer, trivial, inconsequential things that ordinarily hold no meaning. On this occasion it hung upon a mesquite branch.

Though it was the darkest hour of night—that just preceding dawn—and Rio Jack's movements were obscured by the deep shadows, his progress as he fought his way through the thorny tangle could be plainly heard. So loud in fact was the noise he made as he worked his way through the chaparral that even his cat-quick ears could hear no other sound.

A twisted mesquite branch abruptly slapped him across the chin. As he stooped low to pass beneath it a gun exploded almost in his face. The flare of bursting powder nearly blinded him as lead cut past above his crouching form.

His breath sucked in harshly as he realized the narrowness of his escape. Hot blood pounded in his temples. His guns spat flame as the spiked hammers dropped beneath his thumbs. A body fell in the brush beyond, writhed a moment and became still. Slowly the vast silence of the open places came creeping back.

Rio Jack wiped cold sweat from his forehead. There seemed to be a tiny clearing just in front of him. Still gripping the butt of one holstered pistol he struck a match with his left hand. It flared orange against the drifting shadows, illumined the tiny clearing and played fitfully upon the motionless crumpled figure of a man in a steeple-crowned sombrero.

'Rio! *Rio!*' came the girl's frightened voice. 'Are you hurt?'

'I'm all right. Be with you in a couple of shakes.' He bent forward, turned the man over with his foot, alert as a crouching puma.

It was the peon Mexico whom he had first encountered at the Hacienda of the Limping Crow. The man's shirt was sticky with blood where it covered his left breast. But the bleeding had stopped. The man was dead.

Bewilderment twisted Rio Jack's rugged features. How had Mexico gotten here when he had shot the man back in Gunsmoke? Evidently he had failed to score a hit in town. Yet that did not explain how the man came to be here, across the mountains. Had some part of the posse after all managed to cut in ahead of him somewhere?

It seemed impossible, incomprehensible. Yet here was Mexico. The man's presence here could not be denied nor laughed away. If he was here it seemed hardly likely that there were not others of his stripe. And if there were—

Rio Jack shrugged his broad shoulders. Cords of muscle tightened along his jaw. He clenched his big hands ominously. He was thinking, not of the dead man, but of those who were yet to die. This was a tough layout and no mistake, but of one thing he felt certain—he would fight to the last gasp in the service of this girl he had come to love.

For a long moment he stood looking down at the half-breed's silent form. The fellow might have papers of some sort on him, he thought, and bent to search his ragged clothes.

But even as he stooped, he stiffened.

A startled scream sheared through the drifting murk.

Cold prickles of fear swept up the spine of Rio Jack. That scream could come from none but Nita! What could have happened while he crouched here in the thicket? He wasted no time in conjecture but whirling, blazed a headlong path of fury through the clutching brush while the hot blood thundered at his temples.

As he broke clear he could hear the dimming pound of distant horsemen.

Rio Jack stood still, his rugged face a sombre mask. Cold anger tore at him as he listened to the receding thud of vanished hoofs. His lean jaw grew rigid in the darkness as he recalled the trust the girl had placed in him.

Now she was gone—

Rage ripped through him like jagged waves of fire and his grey eyes glowed like polished agate. Wild fury filled his brain and only one coherent thought thrust through it—*he must find and destroy Nevada Ablon!*

The thought was more than a mere subconscious process of the mind; it was a gnawing white-hot desire. For he was quick to realize that none but the lanky renegade knew this country well enough to out-general him. Once again had the wily Ablon thwarted him and escaped unpunished. Rio Jack swore softly that he had done so for the final time.

*   *   *

A golden dawn came swiftly to flood the range with light.

Rio Jack saw now that the level land below was not so near as he had thought. A sluggish mudbrown stream must be crossed before he reached it; a winding, tortuous stream which he guessed to be the Pecos River. In the shadow-dappled distance beyond, the huddled outline of sun-whipped adobes stood naked against the desolate plain. Langtry—the only town in a radius of many miles.

As usual, Ablon had been methodical Rio Jack saw as he glanced about him. His borrowed claybank was gone with the girl and the roan broomtail she had been riding. Ablon had made a clean sweep and vanished. Such had ever been his furtive way. Not that he was cowardly; Rio Jack knew better than that. It was just that the man's scheming, cautious mind had told him there could be no advantage to himself in stopping to cross guns with an hombre of Golden's well-known ability. Upon occasion the lanky Ablon could be as recklessly daring as any man alive. Rio Jack had been afforded ample evidence of the fact during the past four years.

His hard-bitten face held as much expression as a mask a man might chop from wood with a

214

hatchet as his grey glance beat out across the distance that separated himself from Langtry. A swim and a long hard walk stretched out before him. Two thirds of the way towards town his eyes picked out a dustcloud which he knew to be caused by horsemen, for no wind was stirring yet.

'Sure got away to a good start,' he reflected grimly. Taking up the slack in his belt he set off down the slope towards the placid river which, at this point, was but a scant twenty feet in width. Luckily the banks were low, affording easy access to the stream.

As he slipped and slithered downward he attempted to force all thought of the girl and her plight from his mind, but found himself unable. Her piquant face, framed by its lustrous blue-black hair, was ever before his vision, mocking him for her misplaced trust.

'But damn it,' he growled gloomily, 'I couldn't leave that half-breed runnin' loose! Any other gent would have done what I did. How was I to know that orn'ry son was just a decoy?'

Yet wherever he turned his face Juanita's lovely golden eyes were there to mock him. He could not shut her image from his mind. It was there, and there it stayed. It was with him when he swam the river; her eyes watched him as he swabbed the water from his guns and refilled their cylinders with fresh cartridges from the loops of his belts; they danced before him

215

reproachfully as he lurched his limping way across the plain beneath the boiling sun that struck down upon the thirsty earth like the blows of a brassy hammer. Her image was still before him when at noon he staggered into Langtry's single street and made his way to the Lone Star Corral.

The gaunt leather-faced proprietor regarded him curiously. 'Where'd you drop from, pilgrim?'

'Who wants to know?'

'Well, there was a party through here this mawnin' what described a gent that would be a dead ringer for you. Said gent, 'cordin' to this party, has a five-hundred dollar bounty on his pelt,' the fellow answered, fingering his gun-butt.

'You hankerin' to collect?' Rio Jack's wide lips framed a satanic grin.

The man swallowed nervously. 'Not me, Mister. I was just mentionin' the fact casual-like. Thought you might want to know.'

'That's friendly of you. Any other jaspers given that description?'

'I reckon the depity heard it. He was here when the party stopped to change broncs.'

How much of the man's information was true, and how much more there might be that he had not deemed advisable to mention, Rio Jack could only guess. But if a trap had been laid here for him, nothing save constant unremitting vigilance on his part could hope to thwart it.

'I want a good fast bronc, friend—the fastest one you got.'

The man shifted his feet uneasily. 'I'd like to accommodate you, sure,' he said. 'But the truth is them other fellas cleaned me out. All I got here now, outside a crowbait or two, is the nags that other party left. They won't be much good for two-three days.'

Rio Jack's grey glance beat hard against him. 'I don't like to call a man a liar, but you better take another look. What's the matter with that long-legged calico over there?'

'That—that hoss—' the proprietor of the Lone Star Corral ran a nervous tongue across his lips, swallowed and hastily finished, 'belongs to Depity Ike Barlow.'

'Yeah? Well, you slap a saddle on it—quick!'

The man took a final look at Rio Jack's hard-bitten features and departed at a run. Exactly one minute later the pinto stood saddled and ready.

'Listen,' said Rio Jack, speaking around the cigarette he had just rolled. 'Listen. You tell this Ike Barlow hombre that Rio Jack Golden borrowed his horse. Tell him I'll return it in a week or two or send him the money for it. Savvy?'

The man bobbed his head. 'I'll tell him, mister.'

'You better,' Rio Jack said grimly, and swung into the pinto's saddle. '*Adios.*'

He had not asked which way Ablon's party had taken because he realized that he would likely hear a lie. Had he been in Ablon's boots, he would have headed back towards Gunsmoke. But Ablon was a wily hombre, cunning as a lynx. He had always evaded the trap of doing the expected thing. Chances were that he had shoved on towards Dryden and the vast mountainous country to the southwest. So thinking, Rio Jack struck out in the direction at a fast lope.

An hour later he found himself in brushy country. Mesquite, greasewood and cholla studded the rolling range in wild profusion. The legs of his tight *charro* pants were soon ripped to shreds about his knees. He reflected sardonically that he might just as well have commandeered a pair of chaps while he was 'borrowing' the calico pony.

He was flanking a ridge when the pinto put up his ears. Rio Jack's hand shot forward, closing upon the animal's muzzle just in time to prevent a betraying whinny. He caught the muffled thud of approaching hoofs as he brought the pinto to a halt. With his hand still gripping the animal's nose, he waited motionless, his roving glance hard and alert as his cat-quick ears caught fractions of a muted conversation.

Cold dread closed down upon him as he sat rigid in the saddle. It would be hell to be stopped after getting this far on the fugitives' trail!

As the horsemen on the ridge's far side drew nearer, their voices became increasingly clear. Apparently the unknown riders were moving parallel with his own course, but in the opposite direction. A voice came clearly now:

'Hell, he musta taken some other direction, Jabe. Can't see no sense in stickin' round yere no longer. Damn' sun's plumb fried me to a blister!'

'Yeah—me, too! Ablon missed his guess this time sure. Might's well mosey back to town. My belly's been rubbin' on m' backbone for the last hour, I'm s' hungry,' another voice chipped in. 'What say, Ike? Do we fan dust or stick a spell longer?'

'Oh, hell! Let's go back to town.'

Rio Jack sat motionless till the creak of saddle leather, the muffled fall of hoofs and the voices faded out. He sighed then and wiped the perspiration from his face.

'Close shave, horse. I owe you somethin' for that, I reckon.' He gave the animal an affectionate slap and kneed him on.

It must be close to two o'clock, he thought, glancing at his shadow in the manner of range-bred men who have no need for watches. Been a long while since he had eaten. Hearing those fellows mention grub made a gent sort of hungry-like.

Thought of food brought to mind his weariness. He had not slept for hours and

219

hours and the strain, he realized, was beginning to tell. And the hectic adventures of the past few days had taken their toll of his vitality, too. Even his brain seemed numbed by fatigue. And as far as his personal problem was concerned, naught had been accomplished. Ablon still roamed free. He would never feel at peace with his conscience until his score with the fellow was settled.

He would stop at the next ranch he encountered and get a bite to eat, maybe some sandwiches or jerky to take along. He could not stop for rest, badly as he needed it, while Nita remained in the renegade's hands. Time-killing sleep must be staved off at all costs.

An hour later he sighted the adobe buildings of a small spread and turned his horse towards them.

There was no sign of life about the bunkhouse or outbuildings. But at his hail a burly, thick-necked man in faded jeans and flannel shirt stepped from the ranch house with a rifle in his hands. In the doorway behind him stood a grim-faced woman. A wide-eyed boy peered out from behind her skirt.

'Howdy,' the man's tone was non-committal.

Rio Jack's wide lips parted in a weary grin. 'Howdy, *amigo*. Wonder if you could fix me up with a bite to eat, a snack to take along an' a pair of chaps?'

'Travellin' far?'

220

'Headin' for El Paso,' Rio Jack answered after a moment's hesitation. The man looked honest enough. There was a glint of suspicion in his glance that Rio Jack could appreciate. Giving aid to wandering strangers often turned out to be a dangerous business. He decided to be frank: 'I'm known as Rio Jack,' he said. 'The last name is Golden.'

Sudden interest chased the suspicion from the burly man's features. 'Rio Jack! Wal, wal! Glad to know yuh.' He stood his rifle against the house and strode forward, hand outstretched. 'I heard a heap o' yuh off'n on. Ain't often a man gets to meet a gent in yore class. 'Light down an' rest yuh'r saddle, friend. Mary'll fix yuh up somethin' sure.'

There was no apparent hesitation in Rio Jack's manner as he slid from the saddle and gripped the proffered hand. Yet his left was close to its holstered pistol. One never knew— this fellow seemed all right, but plenty of men had gone down while shaking hands with strangers.

The rancher's strong grip was not unduly prolonged.

'Careful, ain't yuh?' he chuckled with a glance at the poised left hand.

'Fellow with my reputation has to be,' Rio Jack answered dryly. 'About them chaps—'

'Reckon I c'n find a pair to fit yuh. Oughta be two-three odd pair in the harness shed.'

They sauntered towards it, a small adobe

221

building behind the bunkhouse. 'Headin' for El Paso, eh? Wouldn't be follerin' the party that shied past here couple hours back, I reckon?'

Rio Jack studied him with a sidelong glance.

'Not aimin' to be curious,' the man said hastily. 'Just thought yuh might wanta know there was five-six horsemen ahead o' yuh. Looked like one of 'em mighta been a girl.'

'Uh-huh? Couple hours back, eh? Travellin' fast?'

'So-so. Not raisin' any lather. Not doin' any stoppin', either. Hard-faced outfit.'

'Yeah.' Rio Jack inspected the worn chaps the other handed him, tried them on. 'Not bad,' he said. 'How much?'

The burly rancher flushed. 'Yuh oughta know better'n that,' he growled.

'My mistake, pardner. Much obliged. Mebbe I can do as much for you sometime.'

'If yuh get a chance to rub out the king-pin o' that party ridin' ahead o' yuh, I'll consider it all the favour any gent could do me.'

'Ablon?'

The man chuckled. 'So yuh *are* trailin' 'em! ... Yeah—Ablon.'

Rio Jack's grin was rueful. 'Got me, that time,' he admitted. But he said no more about the lanky Nevadan. Nor did the rancher appear to expect any further remark.

* * *

Six days later Rio Jack reached San Elizario, a mere handful of miles from El Paso. Six days of hard riding, constantly changing horses; six days of heat and thirst and hunger. He ate when the opportunity occurred, frugally, hurriedly. He snatched what sleep he got in the same manner, often dozing in the saddle when he knew that safety demanded that he constantly be alert.

At San Elizario he learned that Nevada Ablon and his party had crossed the river not three hours before his arrival. They appeared to be heading, his informant told him, for Juarez.

'Was there a girl with 'em—a black-haired girl with golden eyes?'

'Yeah. Dressed like a man, she was, an' lookin' mighty tired. You follerin' 'em?'

'Well,' Rio Jack said guardedly, 'I'm sorta trailin' their way. What makes you think they're aimin' for Juarez?'

'From things the leader let drop when we was talkin'. Seems like they're figurin' to join up with the revolutionists. Villa's camped outside Juarez!'

CHAPTER NINETEEN

DANGEROUS SHADOWS

Rio Jack felt no surprise that Villa had come so suddenly north. The man's actions were not predictable; he was a creature of moods and sudden impulse as the good patriots of Mexico had learned to their sorrow.

But though Rio Jack realized that Ablon would push on to Juarez to-night, he lingered in San Elizario for a meal at the restaurant—his first good feed in days. He ate with slow relish, his grey eyes dwelling with ironic humour on a big Mexican further down the counter. The object of his steady attention was dressed in the garb of a vaquero, and his heavily-bandaged left hand was in a sling. Yet Rio Jack knew him for the gilded man he was—one of the former escort with which he and the girl had set out from Villa's camp.

Ablon had lost none of his cunning, Rio Jack reflected. This Mexican had been left here just in case he had managed to cling to the Nevadan's trail. Ablon wanted no last-minute denouements in front of the impulsive Pancho.

Yet, though he realized perfectly that the Mexican had been left behind to kill him should he succeed in trailing Ablon's party this far, no sign of fear or caution was discernible in

224

Rio Jack's hard-bitten features. The deep strength of him held his face like a mask of bronze, save for the ironic glint in his agate glance.

He finished his meal and strode outside, placing his back to an adobe wall. After a moment the Mexican followed. His right hand whipped up in salute.

Rio Jack chuckled. 'Hi, there, *amigo*. Long time no see.'

The Mexican hooked the thumb of his right hand in a buttonhole of his leather jacket and grinned. He did not speak, but the American saw that the bandaged left hand in the sling swung casually in his direction. Light flared murkily in the Mexican's smouldering eyes. A foul epithet came from his grinning lips.

Jumping aside as flame spurted from the Mexican's bandaged hand, Rio Jack went into action like a coiled rattler. His speed-blurred hands flashed down. Hammers fell beneath his flicking thumbs, sending out a swift tattoo that drowned the echoes of the bandaged gun. Leaden impact flung the Mexican backward like a scrap of paper in a heady breeze, smashed him down. Dust rose above his prostrate form and settled slowly.

Rio Jack's grey eyes lifted to a sea of faces. 'He asked for it.'

'He sure did, fella—an' he got it!' growled a thickset man in store clothes. 'I'm Marshal of this here town an' I seen the whole business.

You can ride any time you please.'

'Thanks.' Rio Jack released the handles of his guns and, taking his tobacco sack from his shirt pocket, commenced the rolling of a cigarette.

'Yes, sir! You can leave any time you're ready, stranger. An' was I you, I'd crawl aboard my bronc pronto an' get busy makin' tracks. This town would take it kindly if you could see fit to move on—before dark.'

Rio Jack's grey glance slewed round obliquely. The sun's molten shape hung low upon the western horizon. Inside ten minutes it would sink from sight. He was being warned to leave immediately.

'Kinda shovin' on the reins, ain't you?' a ribbon of smoke crossed his lips with the words. His eyes were hard and bright.

'I'm tryin' to do you a favour,' the marshal said. 'Last gun fighter to show up here was hung to that there tree inside two hours of his arrival. This town don't like the breed— nothin' personal in it, you understand. We're jest sort of peaceful by nature. We don't care for noise.'

Rio Jack glanced at the tree, a sturdy old cottonwood, and felt a cold chill touch his spine. As the officer had said, there was nothing personal in his ultimatum. Rio Jack had fought in self-defence; for that he was being warned out. Had the Mexican been the survivor of the fracas, he would have been

226

given short shrift. That Rio Jack had been intending to leave town promptly made no difference. It would have been the same had his plans necessitated a stay in this town. He could leave or he could hang, one. The choice was his.

'Folks work fast in this man's town,' he commented.

The lawman shrugged. 'We don't like gun fights. Our medicine works wonders. Do you stay or do you ride?'

Rio Jack grinned mirthlessly. 'I ride if I can get a bronc. Horse I rode in on is pretty well fagged.'

'I got a horse down to the livery that'll suit you to the ground, an' I can let you have it cheap. Fact is,' the marshal added, 'I'll make you an even trade, sight unseen.'

'Is the critter dead?'

The lawman chuckled. 'The last gent that got on him didn't think so!'

They walked to the livery. Rio Jack looked the animal over. Nothing to brag about for speed, he decided, but plenty of endurance. A short-coupled strawberry roan with little pin ears. Weight about eleven hundred pounds. Mean eyes and a Roman nose.

'Is this the nag they wrote the song about?' he asked.

The lawman's eyes twinkled. 'Second cousin, prob'ly. Will he suit?'

'Guess he'll have to. Beggars can't be choosers.'

In three minutes Rio Jack had got his gear and strapped it on the ugly roan back.

'Give my regards t' all inquirin' friends,' he said ironically, and stepped into the saddle. The roan wasted no time in warming up with pitching; he loosened up in a spine-jolting buck-and-swing! Inside of five minutes he had gone through more tricks than most equines had ever dreamed of while the marshal looked on with wooden face. But the easy-swaying Golden stayed right with him, from time to time puffing nonchalantly on the cigarette that dangled from his tight-pressed lips, raking the lunging animal from neck to flanks with his big-rowelled spurs. With a final heave the roan quit cold and stood awaiting the inevitable beating his former master had been in the habit of administering. Rio Jack playfully rubbed the little ears.

'That's ridin', fella!'

'Nice of you to say so,' Rio Jack commented dryly. His insides felt as though they'd been shaken loose of their proper moorings, scrambled, and dumped in a heap at the pit of his stomach. And his surroundings seemed to have been coated with a fuzzy blur.

He got out 'the makings' and began the manufacture of a cigarette. He took his time. Fellow needed something to occupy his hands after five minutes on the hurricane deck of old strawberry roan.

When he could trust his voice he asked

sardonically: 'Ever tried ridin' this broken-down plug yourself?'

'Not me!' The marshal said. 'I got some respect for my health. That bronc's the closest thing to a chunk of ragged lightnin' I ever seen—an' I've saw a lot! Only two gents that's ever rode him was you an' the fella that brought him here; the gent we used to ornament the cottonwood.'

He cleared his throat, took a squint at the darkening western skyline and said suggestively: 'Sun's gone down. Be dark in two-three minutes sure. Guess you'll be anxious to fog along. *Vaya con Dios.*'

'Your solicitude is touchin',' Rio Jack grinned derisively, turned the roan's head and jogged off towards the river.

*   *   *

Ten o'clock found him but a mile or two from Zaragoza, on the Mexican side of the Rio Grande. Conserving his mount had lost him a little time, but not much. He consoled himself with the thought that, due to the general's well-known habit of going early to bed, Ablon would be unable to talk with Villa before morning, no matter what time to-night he arrived at General Headquarters. And much might yet be done before morning.

The thoughtful marshal of San Elizario had provided him with a .30-.30 repeating rifle

229

which was now scabbarded beneath his stirrup leather, its stock within instant reach in case of emergency. Little did he guess, as he picked his way along the trail, how soon the emergency was to arise, or when it did how futile the rifle was to prove.

Soon the trail widened to a rutted road that angled towards the distant hamlet. Stunted brush and giant cactus grew along its edges and flung grotesque shadows across its uneven surface.

Ahead Rio Jack could see a place where the road dropped to a low ravine. The pitch leading down was bright with moonglow, but in the bottom of the gorge was a wide pool of murky gloom.

The wolfish instinct of danger that grows keen in a rider of the lonesome trails abruptly rang a gong of warning in his mind. A sudden sense of menace enveloped him. The flexure of his hand upon the reins stopped the roan at the top of the descent.

His hard grey probing gaze flicked downward towards the gloom but detected no slightest stirring of the shadows. The murky pocket seemed empty as a discarded glove.

'Shucks,' he thought, 'I'm gettin' skittish as a new-foaled colt. Nothin' down there for a grown man to be afraid of. Why, ol' strawberry roan ain't feelin' a mite spooky. Shucks—giddap!' he said and, with a shrug, sent the horse angling down the slope.

Loose shale clattered under steel-shod hoofs. Moonlight fell placidly upon the open rutted road. From the distant south came a lone wolf's mournful howl. But nothing happened and as he drew near the slope's base where the sky's disc silvered the brush and upthrust rocks, Rio Jack chuckled at the sense of fear he had entertained.

But the chuckle suddenly ceased.

A livid streak of crimson tore the gloom. Spurts of flame mushroomed from the heavy shadows. Lead ripped through the wide-brimmed hat of Rio Jack. Lead seared a burning path across his ribs and left him dizzy. Pain almost dropped him from the saddle as white-hot metal grazed his thigh. Another slug struck the saddle horn and splashed, sending the roan into a convulsion of frenzied pitching as the roar of belching guns churned up the raucous echoes.

With strong left hand Rio Jack fought the roan to a shivering standstill while his rope-scarred right dropped to a triggerless gun, swung its muzzle upward. Orange fire spurted from his hip in a pulsing drum of sound that sheared the echoes and sent cold lead ripping through the murk.

A man yelled out in wildest agony. A second swore.

A lithe twisting shape shot across Golden's path and he drove a bullet at it, saw it reel. He flung the big roan forward into the seething

231

shadows with the hot breath of smoking guns in his nostrils. His eardrums rang with smashing reports. The earth jarred and shook beneath the strawberry's hoofs.

A cursing figure sprang up before him with flashing Colt. A hammer dropped beneath his thumb and he saw the man fall away. A horse went down beside him, struck by flying lead. All was turmoil, wild confusion. It seemed as though all the guns in the world were taking part in the fierce din reverberating through the hollow.

Rio Jack saw blurred milling forms before him and drove his roan among them slashing viciously with empty gun. He dallied the reins about the horn and yanked his left gun from its mockery of a holster.

He was in a trap and knew it. Ablon had left the last of his men here to make sure he did not follow further. The trap had sprung and caught him because he had refused to heed the warning of his instinct.

His booming laugh rang out and joined the echoes. He swore no trap of Ablon's devising could ever hold him. He hurled the bucking snorting roan full at the hazy shapes of running men. The impact sent one sprawling. A riderless horse careened madly up the road, was momentarily silhouetted against the skyline before it vanished.

Someone shouted: 'My Gawd! I got enough!' A horse went pounding off among the

232

shadows. The flames of gunfire crisscrossed the gloomy hollow like jagged lightning. Rio Jack, cold as ice in a thing like this, held his fire and waited.

'*Madre de Dios! Vamonos!*' gruffed a husky voice a yard away. Rio Jack let the hammer of his left gun fall beneath his thumb. The man went down with a gasping curse. Rio Jack could hear him threshing on the ground.

'Fight, you dry-gulchin' sons! Fight!' snarled Rio Jack, and strained his eyes against the murk.

But he saw no movement anywhere. Returning silence came creeping slowly to the gorge. The rumbling echoes died away. A flat hush closed down wherein no tiniest insect voiced a sound.

Suddenly as it had started the fight had finished. Rio Jack was left alone.

His hands shook as he punched the empty shells from the cylinders of his triggerless weapons, replaced them with fresh cartridges from his belts. Reaction was setting in. He felt suddenly tired, exhausted. His side throbbed painfully where the bullet had grazed his ribs. Holstering his guns, he slupped a hand inside his bloody shirt, sent exploring fingers across the wound. A mere flesh wound, he decided, not dangerous but painful. He bound it up with strips torn from his shirt and examined the wound in his thigh.

'A scratch!' he said and laughed. It seemed

233

impossible that he should have emerged from the trap alive. He pinched himself. 'But I am!' he said aloud. He laughed some more; loud, booming laughter that yet held a shaky note in it somewhere. His head felt light. He looked at the moonlit slope behind him and laughed again. The damn' hill was reeling like a drunken sailor!

'C'mon, horse,' he muttered. 'Let's get outa this 'fore I go nuts! Whoever heard of a hill that reeled?' he asked, and because no one answered his laugh broke out once more.

He reached Zaragoza at midnight, clear-headed again, but so exhausted from lack of sleep and loss of blood that only his iron will kept him in the saddle. No light showed from shuttered windows. The place was silent as a grave and the bright metallic moonlight washed the walls of the boxlike adobes and made sharp contrasts of white and blue.

He pulled tobacco sack and papers from the pockets of his scarlet shirt and rolled himself a smoke, inhaling deeply. Where he had torn strips from the shirt to bind his wounds the night air brushed chill against him. He felt cold and tired and hungry.

It did not occur to him to thank God he was alive.

His troublous thoughts took another direction. Ablon, he decided, was endeavouring to take those cursed papers to Villa. If he succeeded in placing them in the general's hands Nita's death was both sure and quick to come. By a trick he had originally obtained them from the girl; she had thought him one of Carranza's men because he had things to prove it and the password.

But, having got possession of the papers, he had mocked her with his trick. She had offered him money for their return. Money was Ablon's god; he had accepted. Later, then, after his hurried talk with Villa at that unnamed town below the border, he had endeavoured to steal them back; had succeeded and captured the girl besides, while Rio Jack was stalking the half-breed decoy.

Question was, why was Ablon so anxious now to get the papers to Villa's hands? Whether aid was secured from the United States to run Villa to earth or not could mean but little to the lanky Nevadan. His only allegiance was to himself.

Villa must have offered a mighty tempting reward. Nothing less could have persuaded Nevada Ablon again to cross the trail of the man who had willingly given up four years of his life in an effort to apprehend him.

That must be it, Rio Jack reasoned as he rested. Villa had offered a glittering reward, and Ablon was out to get it.

He must not be permitted to succeed. The fate of Nita hung upon the issue. If Villa got those papers she would be shot as soon as he could call a firing squad. His flaring anger after he read the contents of that bulky envelope might even drive the impulsive general into killing her with his own hand.

Thought of the desperation that must be Nita's drove Rio Jack hurriedly on. What he would do when he reached Juarez did not matter. He would do something—anything necessary to free the girl from her dangerous plight. He could make no plans. His actions would be dictated by what he found when he reached the general's camp. He would free the girl then settle the long outstanding score with Ablon. Nothing mattered after that.

That the girl might care as much for him as he did for her was a thought that never entered his mind. Why should she? He was nothing but a border gunman while she was the daughter of Mexican aristocracy. A daughter of the dons.

Yet he rode with her image in his mind. And he drove the big roan hard.

CHAPTER TWENTY

ABLON HOLDS FOUR ACES

Swinging a wide circle so as to approach Juarez from the west, from which direction Ablon would hardly be expecting him, Rio Jack came in sight of the town just as dawn was brightening the rim of the world.

The expanse of sandy waste surrounding the city of adobe lay grey and lifeless. Swiftly, as he drew nearer, a great array of tents became apparent about the railroad station. Beneath the train shed he could make out a number of trains and a conglomeration of troops; some sitting, some lying down as though in sleep, and still others standing about in gesticulating groups.

Cookfires were sending up their thin spirals of smoke when he arrived at the encampment. No one advanced to bar his way; no suspicious questions were hurled at him. Several soldiers turned to stare curiously, but that was all. The noisy incoherent crowd was busy with its own affairs and plainly saw nothing amiss in the newcomer's presence.

Rio Jack was astonished at this lack of interest. He had expected to be stopped and subjected to a rigid questioning. He had deemed the task of entering Villa's headquarters to be a feat in ingenuity. What sort of a military camp was this where strangers could come and go at will? Why this laxity of discipline? Was this a fair sample of Mexican encampments?

He could not understand it. He had entered the jaguar's lair without let or hindrance. Would his going be made as easy? He strongly doubted it. Especially as he was determined not to leave until Nevada Ablon had paid the price of his temerity. Four years he had willingly searched for the lanky renegade, but he was not minded to spend four more in the same manner! The issue must be settled once and for all before he turned his back upon Manana Land.

In the east the sun was coming up, throwing elongated shadows across the yellow earth, gilding the town's adobe buildings, warming its dusty streets, glancing bluely from the stacked rifles of the soldiers as it climbed the cloudless sky, its rays becoming more torrid with each passing moment.

Making his way through the laughing, loitering soldiers and their slatternly women, Rio Jack kneed his weary roan towards a train that stood on a siding a little apart from its fellows. Nearby a number of *dorados*, resplendent in gold braid and ornaments, squatted about a spread blanket playing cards. None of their faces seemed familiar. Nevertheless he eyed them warily as he approached. They did not even bother to look up; their game enchained their interest to the exclusion of all else.

He was glad they were so absorbed. Perhaps it would make his task a little less difficult. It was not so much the hardship of gaining speech with Villa that he feared; it was the problem of getting himself and the girl away when talk or possible gunplay had ceased. He realized full well that he might never leave this camp alive. But the knowledge did not

238

slow his pace.

Yet, disinterested as the soldiers seemed, his heart beat faster as he passed. Probably they had not been with Villa in that little town to the south where Chico Urristra had been hanged. There was no telling, however, when someone who had might see and recognize him for the general's Colonel Oro. He loosened his heavy pistols in their holsters and pressed the roan onward towards the distant train.

He noted abstractedly as he rode the way the warming sunlight caught, held, and slid across the silver conchos, belt buckles, epaulettes and chains of military groups.

As he neared the private train the soldiers thinned away, leaving only the busy card-players within a radius of eighty yards, aside from the sentry who was lounging half-asleep beside the steps of Villa's private car.

As he stepped from his horse and trailed the reins he could hear the hum of voices. The sentinel sprang erect, hastily dropping the *cigarro* that had been between his lips. He glared frostily at the stranger's dusty garb.

'I'm aimin' to see the Chief, *amigo*,' Rio Jack said easily.

The sentry made no movement, gave no evidence of hearing.

'Been havin' trouble with your ears, *amigo*?'

The sentry stared steadily before him, not even an eye-blink breaking his stoic calm.

'Listen, hombre. I want to see the General—

239

quick!'

The sentry smiled a trifle. It was as though a wooden face had cracked.

'General busy, *señor*.'

'Yeah?' Rio Jack began, when a cold chill brushed against his spine. From inside the private car a voice had risen in anger—the voice of Nevada Ablon!

A swift side-glance showed that the *dorados* were still absorbed in their gambling. Rio Jack stepped forward. The sentry raised his rifle.

'Go tell the General that Colonel Oro is here.'

'*No entiendo*. The General is not to be disturbed.'

Rio Jack's patience snapped. No telling what was going on inside that car. Every instant might be vital to his plans. He must get inside and get there pronto.

The sun's hot smash gave him sudden inspiration. He swayed slightly as though about to faint or fall, reeled past the sentry and around the platform out of sight of the card-playing *dorados*. The sentry, startled out of his wooden calm, sprang after him. From the corner of an eye, Rio Jack saw the man reach out his arms. He whirled and his fist shot up in a blurring arc that ended at the sentry's chin. The soldier's head snapped back, striking the iron grating of the platform. He hung there, poised an instant, then slid to the dust with no other sound than a soft *plop* as his body struck the ground.

Rio Jack went up the steps with the speed of light and in two strides crossed the platform. Shoving open the door without ceremony he entered the general's car. He shut the door softly and placed his back against it.

His left hand flicked tobacco sack and papers from his pocket. He rolled a smoke with steady hands while accustoming his sun-filled eyes to the dimness of the car. Gradually a shadowy group of figures took form before him; he saw the white oval of Nita's face, the golden eyes wide and frightened.

Then drifting from the gloom a silhouette he knew came forward—Villa's. The broad-brimmed hat was shoved far back on his tawny head. As he came striding forward he seemed to swell and grow in bulk until he filled completely the fascinated gaze of Rio Jack, who felt his heart thud crazily, who felt his pulses pound.

The general stopped an arm's length away. Rio Jack awaited the burning impact of angry lead. Then he realized with amazement, with a sudden sense of shock, that the big pistol was not hanging in its habitual place at the general's hip. Pancho Villa was unarmed!

He stared like a country lout. 'Ge— General—' he began, but the general stopped him. 'It is swell to see you, pal! But I knew you would come back! I knew you were no double-crossing swine!'

241

A burning lump came into the throat of Rio Jack; dissolved as a husky voice jeered:

'Sure he come back—back to get the gal an' them precious papers!'

Whirling, Rio Jack beheld his ancient enemy. Eye to eye they stared across the car. Rio Jack's rugged features stony, his eyes unreadable as agates. Ablon's face taut and ugly, the jagged bravo brand of a knife-scar looming white as lightning against the deep mahogany of frowning forehead.

Villa's voice crashed across the silence.

'You know what that damned Ablon tol' me? He said you was tryin' to run out on me, pal! Said you was grabbing the papers and the girl and making dust! The swine!'

Rio Jack's hard-bitten features reflected no emotion, gave no evidence of churning thoughts. Should he admit the truth in all likelihood he would be shot as soon as Villa could lay hands to a gun. He could weave another myth—But none knew better than he that the time for myths was past...

'Ablon told the truth if he said I was aimin' to run out on you with Nita an' the papers,' his voice was toneless, flat. 'I was figuring to do just that.'

Villa's mouth fell open; he stared in stunned amaze. A cloud, as of regret, crossed his restless eyes. Then he grinned.

'Come on, friend. I don't feel like joking. You tell that damned dog he's lying.'

242

'But he ain't. What he told you was the truth. I couldn't stand by an' see this girl shot—I was doin' my damnedest to get her an' her papers away from Mexico. I was tryin' to get them to El Paso,' he added needlessly.

A moment longer Villa grinned as though striving to see the humour of Rio Jack's crazy words. Then the energetic line of his powerful under-jaw shot forward, jutted. It made Rio Jack's blood run cold to meet his eyes, yet he stood his ground with glance unwavering.

'And all that stuff you told me was lies?'

Rio Jack nodded, silent.

'About wanting to join me, too? About wanting to be an officer of my staff?'

Rio Jack found it hard to meet the general's pleading glance.

'Come on, pal—tell me you meant just that.'

Rio Jack stood silent. There was wonder in his heart. He had been expecting an explosion of the general's violent temper. Instead the man was pleading. Rio Jack was bewildered by Villa's unexpected attitude on learning that he had been betrayed. The man was a paradox.

A moment longer Villa's eyes clung searchingly to his. With a grunt the general swung about, began a savage pacing up and down the car, chin on chest, great hands clenched at his sides. When he turned again, there was a black scowl on his heavy face.

'Did you know what was in those papers?'

'No.'

'Do you know now?'

'Yes.'

'Knowing, would you act the same?'

'I reckon I would, sir, things bein' as they are.'

Villa's poise was tense. His restless eyes were filled with wonder, and with something else.

Nevada Ablon's gruff tones broke the lengthening silence as a pond's placid surface would be broken by a hurled rock.

'Yuh jaspers make me sick with all this play-actin' stuff! I want the money I was promised if I recovered the gal an' them papers! An' what I mean, I want it quick an' I want it in gold!'

'Yeah?' Villa's tawny head swung slowly round until his restless eyes came to a sharp focus on Ablon's hawk-like features. 'Well, you keep on wanting a while longer. Right now I got something else to think about.'

'A fella'd think yuh was Gawd A'mighty tuh hear yuh orate!' jeered Ablon.

Villa took two strides towards him, threat in every movement.

Ablon's hands flashed hipward with speed uncanny. Rio Jack caught the rip of steel on leather as his guns came out. The lanky renegade backed slowly till his back was against a wall, his levelled weapons weaving from right to left, holding the group motionless with silent menace.

Ablon's smouldering eyes were filled with hate and derision. His trap-like lips writhed

244

apart in a malignant sneer. 'Yuh missed a bet when yuh forgot tuh strap yore gun on this mawnin', Pancho. Steady, now—*steady*! I'm holding' all the aces in this man's game! Pry that tin safe o' yoren open now an' count me out my money.' He paused, then added jeeringly:

'No need of countin' it—I'll jest take whatever's in there an' let it go like that!'

CHAPTER TWENTY-ONE

BULLETOLOGY

The suddenness of Ablon's play had found Rio Jack unprepared for action. His mind had been still engrossed with the perplexing problem of what Villa would do, now that he knew for certain that Rio Jack had played him for a fool. That the lanky renegade would flash his guns before this business was concluded, Rio Jack had known. But he had not been expecting the play to come so soon.

But his chagrin was hidden from the others. The deep strength of him held his face like a mask of bronze. His cold grey eyes reflected no more emotion than did the smoke that trickled upward from the cigarette between his lips. An air of utter calm enveloped him.

Yet there was nothing tranquil about the heavy face of Villa that hung like a cloud in the smoky gloom. His eyes blazed infernal fury. His dark features flamed with a rage that was terrible to witness. The dread mechanical smile started from the edges of his flashing teeth.

He started forward towards the crouching renegade.

'Pull in yore horns, yuh fool!' snarled Ablon, the guns still weaving in his hands. 'Come another inch an' yuh'll get a taste o' lead!'

The general's forward movement did not stop. In desperation Ablon swore:

'For God's sake, *stop!*'

Villa laughed and his apelike arms flexed hungrily.

Flame spurted from the muzzle of Ablon's left gun. With the deafening report, Villa was whirled half around by a smashing impact. He caught at his desk, steadying himself and straightened slowly. His face had blanched but the dread grin was still in evidence.

The renegade's right gun hung full on Rio Jack.

But Rio Jack still smoked in moveless silence. His lips quirked with sardonic humour as he stared at the hawk-faced Ablon.

'That's right, Nevada. Go ahead an' shoot. Always been your way to do your fightin' when you had a good-sized edge,' he taunted, seeing from the tail of his eye that Nita huddled against the wall beside the down-pulled shades of the windows, a good three feet from the line of fire.

'Go ahead an' shoot. Better get the job wound up while you got the chance. Pancho's boys'll be gettin' here on the double-quick.'

Ablon swore in a husky whisper. Rio Jack could tell by his face that the renegade realized his mistake in firing off his gun. But his wily brain made him dangerous still, more so if anything, as was proved by his jeering retort:

'Don't waste no time countin' on them blasted 'dobe soldiers, fella. They won't be doin' *yuh* no good. Neither yuh, nor the gal, nor Pancho. I'll have the pleasin' chore o' tellin' 'em how Panch killed the gal an' yuh went hawg-wild an' gunned him!'

'An' how you, in righteous indignation, evened up the score by downin' me?'

'Yuh guessed it first pop, fella. Never was a damn Golden I couldn't get the best of—'

'When you had the drop an' a point-blank range!' Rio Jack finished mockingly.

'Hell! I'm keepin' the drop account o' Pancho!'

'Yeah—you're some snake, hombre. I can almost hear your rattles.'

Ablon chuckled raspingly. 'Reminds me o' the time I stopped yore kid brother's clock. He was a right loud talker till I got ready to squeeze the trigger. Changed his tune right sudden then. Crawled on his knees an' begged me not to kill—'

'You're a liar!'

Ablon opened his mouth as though to make

247

some scathing retort, then closed it slowly as he cocked his head to one side, listening.

Rio Jack caught the approaching scuffle of booted feet. Then Ablon spoke:

'Here comes the 'dobe soldiers. Get ready, folks—' His guns came up menacingly as Villa took a tentative step in his direction. A flame lit his smouldering glance.

Rio Jack knew that the time had come. The realization came to him that each incident in the past four years had been leading him inexorably to this final, all-important moment. At last the showdown between himself and Ablon loomed at hand. Now he would either avenge the wanton murder of his brother or like the Kid himself, become but another notch on the scarred butts of the renegade's guns.

A sidelong, spinning leap carried him in front of Villa's weaponless bulk, presenting a shield against the Nevadan's lead. Then his hands slapped leather. His seeking thumbs found hammers. The hammers drove lead whining through the gloom.

A rocking, roaring storm of sound filled Rio's ears with a deafening clamour. Abstractedly he noted the rocketlike bursts of flame that sprang from Ablon's hips. Without volition then he found himself staggering backward from a smashing impact. Hot blood streamed down across his eyes.

But he felt no pain, no emotion, as he squinted through the smoke towards where the strangely distorted face of Nevada Ablon was sliding down the wall. He felt nothing save a great weariness as a blanket of darkness spun itself about him, cradled him softly in its folds of sable silence.

But, suddenly, it seemed, a smear of voices rose about him; arguing voices whose timbre rose and fell, lulled, and rose again anew. Strive as he did he could make out nothing of their meaning. He seemed to be perched on a thunder cloud that rocked and heaved in a rugged storm. Yet those troublous voices floated ever from the rain and sleet and snow.

Then spring came rolling round the hill; at least, he guessed it was spring, because everything was green and the sun played softly on the trees and flowering cactus. Then all this changed and it was summer; the sun grew baleful, searing, blistering and withering all the green stuff from the earth. He seemed to be dissolving in a mighty sweat. He found himself begging for a breath of cooling air. But he went unheard in that welter of steadily arguing voices.

He grew hazy for a spell, then swore in raging temper. Some fiery fiends were shackling chains about his wrists and ankles, great massive chains with monstrous links. Now they were dragging him off his feathery cloud; hauling him inch by fighting inch towards a great open furnace whose blistering heat made him feel like a barbecued steer. With fiendish laughter his mocking captors prodded him with twenty-foot poles whose reaching ends were equipped with flashing tines.

By the flames of the roaring furnace he made out the glistening faces of his tormentors: Silvas; Nevada Ablon; Concho Corva; Daggett Pring and Cimarron Charlie. Silvas's gloating face was alight with ghoulish triumph. 'I got you now!' he howled.

Then up came a swarthy, pock-marked half-breed. He wore tattered cotton pants and an open ragged shirt. He came lurching forward with a rasping laugh. 'Remember me?' he wagged his tangled head in owl-like fashion. 'Many men have killed me yet still I live, for I am Mexico—'

'Get back in hell where you belong!' snarled Rio Jack, and would have struck him but for the chains that weighed him down.

A great hulking silhouette came shambling forward, one ape-like arm knocking the half-breed from his path. 'By God, pal! I thought I'd lost you for a minute!' the hulking shadow boomed. Rio Jack's blood ran cold as he recognized that thundering voice for Villa's. He could see the mechanical smile starting from the edge of the general's teeth. 'Come on, pal—say you wasn't lyin' when you said you wanted to join me, to be an officer on my staff!'

Rio Jack hung his head and tried to back away, but the great chains would not let him. So he stared again at Villa, saying: 'Sorry,

Pancho, but I was.'

He saw the general's mouth drop open in amaze; heard the big teeth clicking shut as Villa strode towards him menacingly. 'What you got against me, pal?' came his booming, deafening growl.

'Don't come another inch' he warned him, trying to collect his scattered wits. With stupendous logic then he explained how it was that he found himself allied against the famous general. 'It was like this,' he told him frankly. 'It all dates back to a night on Satan's Toe when I drove a howling pack of renegades scurryin' down a moonlit trail.'

'Oh—I see,' the general muttered.

'Sure. I knew you would understand, compadre,' Rio Jack assured him earnestly. 'It was the girl, you know. Prettiest girl in a ten days' ride! Those hellions were after her. You know I couldn't let 'em get her. "You get to hell back down that trail," I tells 'em, "or I'll fog you up so bad the Injuns'll be usin' your hides for strainers!"'

The general stared with breathless interest. 'Did they go?'

'Did they? You know damn well they did! Them that was able left so fast you couldn't see 'em for the dust!'

The general nodded as though fully satisfied with this bland explanation. With a parting grin he turned and strode away. But hardly had he gone than from the place where he'd been standing, up sprang the lanky form of the renegade Nevadan, a sneer on his twisted lips, his white scar gleaming, a cocked pistol in either hand.

'I thought I killed you!' cried Rio Jack, astounded.

'*Me!* Hell, there never was a Golden yet could get the best o' me!' the Nevadan jeered. 'I got a notion to wrop yuh round my finger fer a ring!'

'Not man enough,' taunted Rio Jack, and saw the lanky Ablon fire. First one gun and then the other spat livid lines of flame. Fiery hornets screamed about him; they stung his face, his hands, his chest and legs and head. He tried to duck but someone seemed to be clutching him tightly and he could not move—he could not even wriggle.

So he closed his burning eyes to shut the scene away...

*   *   *

When he opened his eyes again, Rio Jack found himself in a tiny place with canvas walls; bright and white it gleamed like shining corded metal. He saw that he was stretched out on a cot and wondered whose it was. He was puzzled, too, as to how he came to be here. Reaching up a shaky hand he found that there was something bound about his head. Then the hand caught his attention and he laughed. The

252

laugh seemed sort of cracked and far away. But the hand—Gosh, that skinny claw could not belong to him!

'By God, pal! I told that crazy pill-roller it would take more than a few chunks of lead to make *you* shuffle off!'

Rio Jack looked up with a wan grin. 'Howdy—Pancho.' He rubbed his chin and found it sort of rough and raspy-like. He flashed the general a startled look. 'Say! how long have I been here?'

'Twelve days,' said Villa, grinning. 'And every blasted day that fool saw-bones says, "To-morrow he will die!" But you showed him, pal! I knew you wouldn't croak!'

Rio Jack moved his head experimentally. Still working, he found. But twelve days! Must have been shot up pretty much, he reflected grimly. Then a sudden thought chased all personal considerations skallyhooting.

'Say!' he got an elbow under him and raised his body slightly. 'What about them papers you been after?'

Villa laughed. 'I tore them up. And— thanks, pal, for the way you jumped in front of me when that swine Albon fired. I'm going to make you a general!'

'Not me, *amigo*!' though weak, Rio Jack's tone was emphatic. 'I got enough fightin' to last me the rest of my natural! Did Ablon get away?'

'Where he got he's raising blisters with a

253

pitchfork!' Villa growled. 'You gave him enough lead to start a pencil factory!' He stared at Rio Jack admiringly. 'I'm going to make you a general, pal—'

'Not while I'm in my right mind!' Rio Jack's tone was final. 'I ain't got a thing against you personal, but—Heck! You see my angle, don't you?'

'I can see a certain filly has you wrapped around her finger,' Villa said, then added reflectively, 'Women sure raise hell with any man's war.'

Rio Jack lay silent, thinking. At last he ventured:

'Uh ... er, how is she, General?'

'She's all right. You know that fellow Silvas? Him an' one of his deputies got into a argument an' shot each other all to splatters!'

'Never mind that. Where's Nita? I'd like to see her—'

'Don't think you ought to, pal. That sawbones said to keep you quiet and restful.'

'You send her in here pronto,' Rio Jack threatened, 'or I'll get up an' hunt her!'

Villa left with a chuckle. The minutes dragged. Rio Jack closed his eyes to summon strength for the coming ordeal. It would be an ordeal, he knew, for he had never been much of a hand at parlour conversations. He knew what he wanted, but had no idea how to put the thing in words.

Approaching footsteps jerked open his eyes

and drew them to the open tent-flap. Nita stood before him, eyes large and wistful. A poignant silence hung between them. He could find no words to break it. He wanted to tell her how her golden eyes had haunted him ever since that night at Satan's Toe; wanted to tell how much he loved her, wanted her, desired her for his very own. But all he finally said was:

'Howdy, ma'am ... You're—you're lookin' well.'

'Thank you. I'm leaving to-day—'

'*Leaving!*' he shouted, filled with wild alarm.

'I'm going back to Mexico City,' she explained. 'My work is over here. Villa tore the papers up; made me promise to leave a soldier's business to a soldier. He is letting me go free—'

'Sure. Pancho's a swell hombre. But look—I don't want you to go gallivantin' off! I—I—I been thinkin' how nice it would be if—if— Damn it! I know I'm ugly as galvanized sin an' tongue-tied as a lockjawed polecat, but— What I mean is—is—'

With flaming face he came to a floundering stop.

Nita's face looked awful white, he thought. Kind of like she'd eaten something that didn't set well on her stomach. He hoped she wouldn't faint or anything. Gosh, he'd sure made one awful mess of things!

He stared at the tent's white walls, at the ridgepole, at his hands and the thin blanket that covered him. He was feeling mighty miserable, he told himself, while perspiration stood out upon his forehead in tiny beads.

He stole a sidelong glance at her and stiffened. She was laughing at him! Yet he could not really find it in his toughened heart to blame her. After all, what had he to offer a girl like her?

She was speaking again. He loved to watch the way her white teeth sparkled behind the redness of her lips. Then he got a glimmering of what it was she was saying, and he snapped to abrupt attention. She laughed. 'About time you came out of that trance. Ride that trail again, will you? I'm not sure that I actually caught your meaning.'

'Huh? Oh! Hell, I ain't in no mood t' be run on.'

'Come on, cowboy—spill that line again. And take it slow and fine-like.'

Rio Jack reared up on his elbow and the hot blood went pumping through his veins. 'Come here ... you little devil!'

She came, hesitantly, though her eyes still had their twinkle.

'Kneel down here beside this cot where I can meet you eye to eye.'

She knelt and he said huskily:

'I ain't the kind t' cut much of a figure at this love habla. But I'm crazy as a wall-eyed bronc about you, an'—an' damn it! Will you marry me, or not?'

'Why sure! What can I lose?'

Anything further she might have said was stopped by the rough pressure of his lips upon her own.

We hope you have enjoyed this Large Print book. Other Chivers Press or G. K. Hall Large Print books are available at your library or directly from the publishers. For more information about current and forthcoming titles, please call or write, without obligation, to:

Chivers Press Limited
Windsor Bridge Road
Bath BA2 3AX
England
Tel. (01225) 335336

OR

G. K. Hall
P.O. Box 159
Thorndike, Maine 04986
USA
Tel. (800) 223–6121 (U.S. & Canada)
In Maine call collect: (207) 948–2962

All our Large Print titles are designed for easy reading, and all our books are made to last.